Undercover

Hilda Stahl

Cover Illustration by Ed French

Dedicated with Love
To
the Richardsons
Greg, Kathy, Sean, Jason, Ginger, Tommy Jo
and even Violet

Chapter 1

Molly spun on her heels and faced Dale as he backed against the cash register. "Dale, I can't understand why you refuse to help me get an interview with Quinn Mathis! Since you and I are practically engaged I'd think you'd want to use your influence to help me get in to see him!"

Dale flushed and glanced around the housewares department. "Keep your voice down, Molly. Do you want me to get fired? You know I've been on edge since Quinn took over here." Dale lowered his voice. "I don't want you bothering Quinn after all his trouble."

"Bothering?" Molly forced back the rush of anger. "I am a newspaper reporter. It is my job to get the news. The Mathis family is still news even two months after the *accident*."

Dale frowned. "You can't believe it was anything more than an accident, Molly. Of course it was an accident!"

"How can you know, Dale? No one really knows. But I'm going to find out."

"Reporters should leave that family alone—should leave Quinn Mathis alone. I wouldn't want anyone questioning me if my brother and his wife had died in a car accident only two months ago."

Molly caught Dale's hand. "Please help me,"

she whispered. "It means so much to me."

He shook his head. "I can't. I can't do anything that would get me fired. I need this job."

"Dale, I am *going* to get an interview with Quinn Mathis today no matter how much you object!" Molly's blue eyes flashed. The honey-brown curls of her long hair bobbed around her slender shoulders to touch the thin straps of her yellow and pink flowered sundress. "The right article about Quinn Mathis would be front cover copy and would carry my by-line. Maybe the article would be picked up by the syndicated press."

Dale groaned. "Don't do it, Molly."

She studied Dale thoughtfully. "Secretly maybe you want me to fail so that George Bailer will fire me from the *Freburg News*. I know you have a low opinion of reporters."

"Reporters can be pushy and you know it."

She sighed and nodded. "But I'm not. Not really. I'm determined, but not pushy."

He didn't say anything and she knew he didn't agree. She looked down at her yellow sandals. Maybe if she wasn't a reporter he'd agree to set their wedding date.

Abruptly she pushed the thought aside. Dale loved her and would never want her to fail at her career. Surely he wanted her to be as happy with her job as he was with his as department head of household items at Ardetts. "Please help me get in to see Quinn Mathis, Dale."

"No." Dale tugged at his blue striped tie. "Besides, I only work here. He's the boss. I don't have any pull with him."

"You told me that he respects you. He'd believe you if you told him that I wouldn't distort the truth." She glanced at her watch. "I have an appointment to talk to Al Wilkens at Wilkens' Appliances about the break-in last night, and then I want to come back to Ardetts to talk to Quinn Mathis."

"He's too busy with interviews today. He's looking for a nanny for Steve's daughters. He wouldn't have time to see you even if I did try to get you in."

"We'll see." Somehow she would get the true story behind Steve Mathis's fatal car accident. Again she glanced at her gold watch and her stomach tightened. She really didn't want to face Al Wilkens. She had seen him interviewed on TV and had almost asked George to let someone else take the job. "I must go, Dale. I'll be back."

Dale touched her arm lightly. "Molly, I won't help you see Quinn. I mean it."

She stiffened. "All right, Dale. But don't try to do anything to stop me." She clutched her yellow purse, and walked away, her head up and her back straight.

Molly stopped at the wide glass doors, whispering a quick prayer for help to face Al Wilkens and taking a deep, steadying breath. Then she walked out of the store and to the yellow Mustang that her parents had given her for college graduation four years ago. The Mustang had been five years old at that time and now it was questionable whether or not it would start.

She patted the fender as she walked past to open the door. Heat rushed out and she gasped. "Someday I'll have a car with air." She wrinkled her nose. "A car that runs without stalling would be nice too."

Well, at least she'd had her muffler replaced recently. Starting the car without any trouble, she pulled out behind a white Chevy and drove the few blocks to the appliance store. It would be interesting to talk to Al Wilkens about the break-in, but she hated dealing with such a foul-mouthed person. As a good reporter, she liked people and was never shy with them. It was fun to get perfect strangers to open up and tell her things that they hadn't planned to tell.

Pulling into a parking space beside a red pickup with a dented fender, she glanced in the mirror, dabbed perspiration off her upper lip and smiled at her image. Dad called her his bright butterfly and Mom often said she couldn't believe that she'd mothered such a beautifully magnificent girl.

The Mustang's door squawked as she swung it open and she clicked her tongue and frowned. "Another thing to have fixed," she said.

Exhaust fumes stung her nose and heavy traffic on the street sounded extra loud.

Her heels tapped lightly on the pavement as she hurried toward the door of the small appliance store. The hot sun radiated off the pavement, burning through the thin soles of her yellow sandals. Perspiration dotted her forehead and upper lip as she stepped gratefully into the air-conditioned store. A bell tinkled and a short, stocky man stepped forward. Shelves holding toasters, mixers, can openers and other small appliances lined the walls. The room smelled of cigar smoke.

"May I help you?" The man smiled a plastic smile. She wondered how long he would last if he worked at Ardetts. Dale had often said that Steve Mathis, and now his brother Quinn, insisted on a warm, genuine greeting for all customers.

She stepped forward. "I'm Molly DuPree. I have an appointment with Al Wilkens."

"Oh, yes, yes. Right through that door."

"Thank you."

The man turned away with a grunt.

Molly opened the door and walked through a narrow hall to a closed door marked PRIVATE. Cigar smoke hung heavily in the air. She wrinkled her nose and fanned her hand in front of her face. Canned semi-classical music played softly, sounding out of place in the shabby hallway.

Molly flipped back her long honey-brown curls, dabbed her forehead with a tissue from her purse, then knocked. At a gruff invitation she opened the door and stepped inside a small room with a large desk, chair and file cabinets. The worn brown carpet muted her steps as she walked to the desk and stopped beside a folding chair. The man behind the desk stood slowly and eyed her up and down, then chuckled under his breath. He was middle aged, tall and broad with a bald head and shaggy brown mustache that he licked, then rubbed. His gray eyes flashed with interest, then narrowed as she pulled out a small tape recorder.

"So, you're Molly DuPree! Young and pretty the way I like 'em."

Her skin crawled and she wanted to walk out, but she sank to the chair and set the recorder on the desk between them. "I understand that your store was burglarized last night at eleven-twenty."

"That's right, babe."

Her jaw tightened. "What was taken?"

"Plenty." He motioned with a fleshy hand as he sat on his padded brown plaid chair. Touching his fingertips together, he made a tent with his hands and studied her with narrowed eyes. "Are you sure you're an experienced reporter? I don't want no amateur writing this."

"George Bailer sent me, and he knows his business!"

"No need to snap. You talk nice to me and I'll tell

you all you want to know and more."

She wanted to walk out, but she wanted the story more. Folding her hands over the purse in her lap, she inquired, "What was stolen? Give me as many details of the robbery as you can."

He looked at her hair and her full red lips, then up and down her slender body. "You're a beauty, all right."

"If you're finished looking, answer me."

The grin vanished. "No need to snap." He cleared his throat. "About six thousand dollars' worth of merchandise and five hundred dollars in cash was taken." He went into detail about the items and what a rotten time for him to be in such a bind. From time to time he interjected a suggestive remark that she ignored. He spread out his hands and shrugged his thick shoulders. "Who knows how long the insurance company will take to settle this?"

"Where were you at the time of the robbery?"

His dark brows met over his large nose. "What do you mean, where was I? That's a dumb question to ask. What does it matter where I was?" He suddenly leaned forward, licked his mustache and rubbed a hand across it.

She pushed the recorder closer to him and he immediately leaned back. "Are you trying to upset me so that I forget to get an answer to that question? Do you have something to hide about last night?"

"No. No, of course not." He cleared his throat. "I was at home watching TV and eating a bowl of popcorn."

"Does your insurance cover the robbery?"

"Of course."

"The police report said the back window was broken. Don't you have an alarm system?"

He pushed himself up and strode around the

desk. "You know, you're a real cutey."

Anger churned inside her, but once again she forced it back. "Stay on the subject, Mr. Wilkens."

"Al. Call me Al."

"Mr. Wilkens, tell me about the alarm system." She saw his jaw tighten and it pleased her.

"It wasn't on."

"Does the insurance still cover you?"

"Why wouldn't it? The alarm didn't go off. I don't know how it got turned off." He stepped closer and squeezed her shoulder. She pulled away, but he kept his hand in place.

She turned her head and stared up at him. "Move it or lose it."

He laughed and dropped his hand. Backing away, he tugged at his shirt collar. "You're awful touchy. I was only being friendly. If you get my meaning."

"I get it all right and you'd better believe the readers will get it, too." She stood, dropped the recorder into her purse and swung around, but before she could reach the door, he blocked her way. Flames shot from her blue eyes. "Get out of my way," she said between her teeth.

"Don't act high and mighty with me, lady. I'm bigger and stronger than you."

"Unless you want me to print what's going on right now, you'd better let me go."

He eyed her up and down, realized she meant what she said and stepped aside.

She opened the door, forcing her hand to stay steady against the knob. She would never let him see how agitated she felt. With her head high she walked through the store and onto the sidewalk. Bright red spots colored her cheeks and her ears rang with anger. A car honked and drivers shouted back and forth. Heat rays drifted up from the sidewalk. Perspiration wet her face. With a tired sigh she walked to the cafe next door. She had to sit down and relax before she could drive back to Ardetts.

Smells of coffee, fresh rolls, and baking pies filled the small cafe. Thankfully she sank to a hard bench in the air-conditioned room and leaned her head against the back of the booth. She'd have an icy Coke, visit the washroom to put herself in order, and then go see Dale again. Somehow she had to push Al Wilkens out of her mind.

"May I take your order?"

Molly looked up. A teenager stood there with a pad and pencil poised and ready. Her uniform made her look more like a candy striper in a hospital than a waitress. Her eyes were wide and green and scared, and her thin face was pale. Molly smiled, wondering what was behind the girl's fear. "A small Coke, please."

The girl nodded and turned away without writing anything on the pad. Molly tugged a white napkin from the holder and slowly folded it into a tight square. She moved the salt and pepper shakers closer to the sugar jar. She twisted her diamond and ruby ring around and around on her finger, then fingered her yellow earrings. She took a deep breath and slowly let it out. She forced her thoughts off Al Wilkens and on to Dale. Maybe he'd change his mind and get an interview with Quinn Mathis for her. Wrinkling her nose she shook her head. Once Dale made up his mind, nothing could change it.

"Here's your 7-UP." Her hand trembling, the waitress set the glass down, spilling a little beside the folded napkin. She grabbed another napkin and sopped up the spill. "I'm so sorry! Really I am!"

"That's all right." Molly looked at the glass, then up at the girl. "You brought me the wrong order. I asked for Coke."

"You did?" The girl closed her eyes with a moan and bit her bottom lip.

"Please take this back and bring me a small Coke."

The girl swayed, her face even whiter. "Oh, please. I can't." She dropped her voice. "If I make one more mistake today, I'll be fired and I need this job." She sounded desperate and Molly didn't have the heart to make trouble for her.

"Just bring me a Coke and I'll pay for both drinks."

"Oh, thank you!" The girl hurried away and was soon back with a Coke.

"Why don't you sit down with me and drink the 7-UP?"

The girl shot a look toward the back of the cafe. "Do you really want me to?"

"Yes." Molly smiled and her blue eyes softened as she touched the girl's icy hands.

"I'll wait on the girls coming in now and then go ask. I'll be right back."

A few minutes later Molly sipped her Coke as she watched the waitress gulp down the 7-UP. "I'm Molly DuPree."

"Billie Lane." She smiled uncertainly. "Thanks for not giving me away to Mrs. Peek. She's hard to work for. Do you work, or are you in college?"

Molly shook her head with a low laugh. People often thought she was still in college. "I'm a reporter for the *Freburg News*."

"You are? That's terrific! I'd like a job like that. I bet it's never boring, is it?"

Molly shrugged. "I suppose it is at times, but I love it, so I don't mind."

"Are you married?" Billie glanced at Molly's ring finger.

Molly rubbed her empty finger. "Not yet, but

planning to be."

Billie's face lit up. "Me, too! Just after I'm out of high school. I don't have a boyfriend yet, but I'll get one. I can't wait to have a home of my own away from all my brothers and sisters. It's hard living in a big family. Especially when there's not much money."

"I'm an only child. And that was lonely."

The hum of voices from the booth beside Molly and the music from a radio faded further into the background as Molly talked with Billie. Suddenly Billie jumped up, all the color that had come into her cheeks draining away.

"I must get back to work! Oh, I hope I didn't take too much time off!" She took two steps away, then dashed back. "Thanks for everything, Molly. I won't forget you. I mean it."

"Enjoy your day, Billie. I'll stop in to see you again."

"Would you? That's great!"

Molly watched Billie rush to wait on a customer who had just sat down. Too bad Billie had to work here. Molly frowned thoughtfully. Maybe she could suggest that Billie see Quinn about being a nanny for his two nieces.

A wonderfully daring thought popped into Molly's head. She gripped her purse, her heart racing. Should she apply for the job herself? She could disguise herself, get an interview with Quinn for the job and then get her story.

Her nerves tingled. She paid her bill and walked out into the glaring sunlight.

"I'll do it!" she said.

She laughed softly and nodded. During the interview, she'd find a way to interview the elusive Mr. Quinn Mathis about the accident.

Slowly she drove to Ardetts, her mind whirling with plans.

A few minutes later her stomach tightened as she stopped in front of Ardetts' show window. Would she really go to such lengths to get an interview? She'd promised herself as a Christian reporter that she wouldn't do anything underhanded. She shrugged. This was only an undercover job, and she wouldn't be doing anything wrong. She would get an honest story that wouldn't harm anyone. She wouldn't take the job as nanny to the girls, but she would get an interview.

She sailed into Ardetts, laughing at what she'd have to do to herself so that no one recognized her. With her years of theater training, she could easily apply makeup to make her look different. She'd dress in a style of clothes that she never wore.

But was it right?

She frowned and thrust the thought aside. God understood how badly she needed this story.

Several minutes later Molly stood outside Quinn Mathis's top floor office. Makeup toned down the healthy flush of her skin and made her look pale. A white cotton blouse was buttoned up to her chin and tucked neatly into a plain tan skirt. She wore brown loafers and carried a plain brown purse. Her mass of hair was pulled into a tight knot at the nape of her neck, showing ears that stuck out a little too far. She pushed the large, slightly-tinted glasses up on her nose. Even her best friend wouldn't recognize her today.

She had called, making an appointment at twelve under the name of Molly Lynn. Lynn was her middle name so she wasn't really lying. Quinn Mathis had seen her only once at an Ardetts' picnic several years ago, but he'd never remember her, never connect plain Molly Lynn with flamboyant Molly DuPree.

"I'm going to get an interview with Quinn Mathis!" she muttered with a firm shake of her head. "Even if I have to take the job as nanny." She clapped her hand to her mouth. Would she go that far?

"Would I?" she whispered hoarsely.

She took a deep breath, and slowly nodded.

Just then the elevator doors slid open and Dale stepped out a few feet from her. Her heart plunged to her feet and she frantically looked around for a place to hide. There was none and she stood like a statue. She couldn't burst through the door of Quinn Mathis's outer office as if a lion was after her.

Dale nodded to her absently and continued down the hall toward another door.

She leaned against the wall, her legs weak. Even Dale hadn't recognized her, so neither would Quinn Mathis nor his secretary.

Finally Molly reached for the doorknob.

Chapter 2

Molly stopped just inside Quinn Mathis's outer office and forced back the butterflies fluttering in her stomach. She moistened her full bottom lip and slowly walked toward the attractive gray-haired woman who sat behind a small oak desk. Soft music played in the background. A small flowered couch graced one paneled wall. Two padded arm chairs stood against another wall with a small table between them. Dusty rose was the predominant color with red as an accent. Molly's eyes sparkled with appreciation. She could easily have chosen the color scheme and the decorations. But no one must guess it or she'd never be able to pass as the small brown mouse that she was pretending to be.

Without speaking Molly stopped at the desk. Her usual entrance into a room sparkled with energy and enthusiasm, but this time she stood with her head slightly bowed and her eyes downcast, her purse crushed between her hands.

"May I help you?" The woman flashed a warm, encouraging smile.

"I have an appointment with Mr. Mathis." Molly kept her voice low and hesitant. "I'm Molly Lynn."

"Do I know you? You look familiar to me."

Molly's blood froze. She had been in the office several times requesting an interview with Quinn

Mathis. "We could've run into each other shopping or maybe at church."

"Possibly. I'm Ms. Blaine, Mr. Mathis's private secretary. Have a seat. He'll be right with you."

"I hope I haven't come at a bad time." Molly glanced at the Timex watch that she'd bought just a few minutes earlier for her disguise. Finally the panic eased away and she glanced again at Ms. Blaine. "I know it's lunch time. I wouldn't want to stop Mr. Mathis from eating."

"Don't worry about that, Miss Lynn."

Molly sank to the edge of the couch and sat with her knees together and her purse on her lap, her feet flat on the floor and her hands locked over her purse. Could she really go through with this? It wasn't too late to run out and come back later as herself.

No, she couldn't do that. Quinn Mathis had turned down an interview with her several times in the past few weeks. It must not happen again! Come what may, she'd get the interview with him and she'd learn the true story behind his brother's death.

The intercom buzzed and Ms. Blaine said, "Miss Lynn, Mr. Mathis will see you now." Ms. Blaine walked around her desk. She was tall and slender, almost thin, and dressed in a light gray skirt and white silk blouse with several strands of iridescent beads draped around her neck. "Come this way, please."

"Thank you." Slowly Molly walked across the thick carpet. In just a few seconds she'd stand before Quinn Mathis! Shivers ran up and down her spine and she ducked her head to hide the triumphant sparkle in her eyes. Even if she didn't get the job, she'd ask him questions that anyone at a job interview would ask. Occasionally she'd slip in something else. But would she have enough time to learn all she wanted to know for her story? Suddenly she realized that she did indeed want the job as nanny in order to uncover what she needed to learn for a truly great story.

Ms. Blaine touched her arm and said in a low voice, "Don't be afraid. Mr. Mathis is a very nice man."

"Thank you." Could she really do this to them, to herself? What would happen when he discovered her true identity? Well, she would make sure he never did.

She stepped inside the plush office. Attractively arranged were a large desk, leather sofa and chairs, and a computer. Quinn Mathis rose and walked around the desk and Molly's breath caught in her throat. He was even more handsome than his brother Steve had been. There was something else that caught her attention. He had an air about him that sent her pulse leaping. He was tall with a big frame and not a spare ounce of flesh. His dark hair was brushed back off his wide forehead. Dark brown eyes with flecks of gold were studying her thoughtfully as if he could see beneath her disguise. She stood very still, unable to speak for a moment.

He smiled, showing even white teeth, and her stomach muscles tightened. "Hello, Molly Lynn. I'm Quinn Mathis." He extended his hand and hers trembled as his closed around it. Shivers of awareness flew up and down her spine. Quickly she pulled free before he could feel her tremble.

What was wrong with her? No man had ever affected her this way. Could he hear her heart hammering?

"Please, sit down, Molly."

She sank to the edge of a dark leather chair that smelled wonderful.

Quinn leaned back against his desk, his ankles crossed, his hands supporting him. "Now, tell me, Molly, what experience do you have with children?" His voice was deep and pleasant, but his eyes were watchful.

She met his look, glad that she had tinted lenses to hide her eyes. "I've babysat since I was twelve and I taught a primary girls' Sunday School class for several years. For a while I was a preschool teacher and a kindergarten substitute teacher. I love children, and they like me." Thankfully that was all true.

"Where did you work last?"

Panic rushed through her and she couldn't speak for a moment. She cleared her throat. "To tell you the truth, I haven't worked with children for a while now. I . . . I've been trying to break into writing. But it just didn't . . ." She let her voice trail away.

"It didn't pay off well enough, so you must supplement your income. Is that it?"

She nodded slightly, and forced back a flush of guilt.

"Don't be embarrassed about that. I think it's admirable that you want a career in writing. I've often thought of writing myself."

"You have?" The words popped out and she pulled back into herself and added in a carefully controlled voice. "Fiction or nonfiction?"

He smiled and shrugged one muscular shoulder. "I'm sure you wouldn't be interested."

If only he knew! "I understand that you have been here only a few weeks, Mr. Mathis. Do you enjoy it here?"

"Yes. I'm in charge of our store in Madison, but this is the main store and we felt it would be better for me to be here." Abruptly he stood and walked around his desk to the massive high-backed chair.

His navy blue suit jacket fit snugly across his wide shoulders. Molly could smell a faint aroma of his aftershave and she liked it. He fingered his tie as if he wanted to tug it free. "Molly, I need someone for at least six months. Could you commit yourself to that?"

Six months! What could she say? If she couldn't agree to that, she would never get the job. But, if she did agree, she would have to walk away after she'd gotten the interview from him. He would be very angry. Could she handle his anger or the fact that she'd broken her word?

"I can see your hesitation. I'm sure you'll have enough free time to write, if that's what's stopping you."

She moistened her dry lips with the tip of her tongue. "I could agree to six months." How angry Dale would be to learn about this! "I would need time to write."

Quinn folded his large hands on his desk and leaned forward. "You'd have time. The girls are easy to take care of. Tonya is eight and Deanie seven. They're young and impressionable. Their parents' death almost crushed them and they're not over it yet. They'll need love and patience and understanding."

"I was so sorry to hear about the accident that killed them. It was an accident, wasn't it?" She saw his quick look and frown, and she lowered her dark lashes. "I had heard that it wasn't."

"Rumors fly around like crazy when there's been a death. Don't concern yourself with rumors." He rubbed his jaw and Molly saw a haunted look in his eyes before he blocked it from her. "My mother has been taking care of the girls for the past several days, but she's in charge of our store in Lansing and she can't be away from there much longer."

"I would like the job, Mr. Mathis. I'd be good at it."

"Are you married?"

"No."

"Engaged?"

She hesitated a fraction. "No."

"Would you be able to live in?"

Would she have free time for Dale? She couldn't think about that now. "Yes. That would be no problem."

He picked up a yellow pencil and studied it as the soft background music played. He cleared his throat, then he looked at Molly sharply. "I do need to talk about a very sensitive subject."

"Oh?" She crossed her shapely legs and rubbed her skirt nervously over her knees. His eyes never left her face.

"It would put the two of us together often and that could cause a problem if we allowed it to."

"How is that?"

He hesitated and she could see him searching for words. He cleared his throat again. "I do not welcome unwanted attention. I had to let the last girl go because she had the silly notion that she was in love with me. I don't want that to happen with you."

Her temper shot through the high ceiling, but she managed to sit still and not speak. Oh, the nerve of the man! The arrogance!

"I know that I've embarrassed you, Molly, and I'm sorry."

She let that go as she slowly stood. She didn't speak until he rose. "Mr. Mathis, you really don't have to worry about my falling in love with you. I must admit that you are a very attractive man, but I'm sure I can contain myself." Could he hear the anger in her voice? Was it showing in her eyes?

"I'm sure you can," he said stiffly.

"You are a wonderful catch, I'll have to admit."

"Yes, well . . ."

"And charming."

He tugged at his tie.

"To put you more at ease, I am in love with a wonderful man, so you have nothing to fear from me." She forced a smile. "And he is in love with me."

"That does make it better all the way around."

"Yes, it does." She gripped her purse so tight her fingers ached. "I would not do anything to hurt the man I plan to marry."

"You said you weren't engaged."

"Not yet. We're saving enough money to marry next year."

"Very sensible."

She lifted her chin a fraction. "He might get the wrong idea after he learns that I'm working for you and he sees what a fine catch you are." She saw a muscle jump in his jaw. "I would like you to write a note stating that you have no personal designs on me whatsoever. That would assure everyone all the way around, wouldn't it?"

He ran a finger around the inside of his collar. "I don't think we have to go that far, Molly."

She shrugged. "Perhaps you're right."

"I need someone later today, or no later than tomorrow morning." He named a price that he would pay per week and she bit back a surprised gasp. "I want to offer the job to you."

"I'll take it." She kept the excitement from her voice. "I can be at your house any time you say."

He handed her a card. "I've taken over the family home. Here's the address and private telephone number. I'll be there about six. You can come at seven and I'll personally introduce you to the girls."

She nodded. This was going to be the easiest job she'd ever had. As long as she found a way to get information from him, she would accomplish her purpose. Somehow she'd find a suitable story to tell Dale and her parents. Fortunately Mom and Dad were in Arizona for several weeks.

"Pack a swimsuit. The girls are learning to swim, but they need help. Do you swim?"

Thinking of the awards she'd received in school, she merely nodded. "I can manage enough to keep them safe." She thought of her bright red suit with the bold white trim and decided she would buy a dull, lifeless suit for his sake. "I'll see you about seven, Mr. Mathis."

"Yes. At seven." He absently opened the door and seemed to forget her existence even before she walked out. He closed the door and Molly just stood there.

Ms. Blaine looked up, her fine brows raised questioningly. "Is something wrong? Shall I get you a glass of ice water?"

Molly shook her head. "No, thank you." She forced her voice to sound cheerful. "I got the job. I start this evening."

"I'm pleased for you."

"Thank you." Molly managed a slight smile, then walked out of the office into the quiet hallway. She gritted her teeth and forced the anger back. How she wanted to march right back inside and tell Quinn Mathis that she didn't want the job, that she wanted an interview. She jabbed the elevator button and waited, tapping her toe impatiently. "How dare he think I'd fall for him!"

The elevator doors opened smoothly and she stepped inside, glad that it was empty. She closed her eyes and leaned weakly against the hand rail.

Right now she needed Dale to hold her close. When the elevator stopped, she walked to the nearest restroom. With an unsteady hand she wiped off her makeup and applied her usual blush and lip gloss, pulled the pins from her hair to let it tumble down around her shoulders. She unbuttoned her blouse two buttons down to show off the fine column of her neck and the gold pendant gleaming against her skin.

A few minutes later she walked to housewares, looked up and down the rows of china, cookware, silver and small appliances, then finally spotted Dale near the pewter. She liked the way he styled his blond hair. He was dressed in a light blue suit and white shirt with a tie that matched the blue suit exactly. His chin was a little too small to make him really handsome, but then, who could have the firm chin that Quinn Mathis had?

Dale casually glanced her way, then smiled slightly.

"Hi," she said.

"Why are you here?"

"I told you I had to talk to Quinn Mathis."

Dale gripped her arm, his face flushed. "I told you to leave him alone, didn't I?"

"But I need the story."

Dale dropped his hand. "Am I going to be embarrassed by what you write?"

"Why should you be?"

"He's my boss."

"So?"

"And everyone knows you and I are going together." Dale rammed his hands into his pants' pockets and jangled his change and keys. "At times I don't understand you at all!"

"I don't think you try to, Dale." His words

wounded her, and she forced back the tears that pricked her eyes. "I'm only doing my job."

"This is not the place to get into a personal conversation. I'll see you as we planned for dinner."

She bit back a moan. She'd forgotten about their date. "I'm sorry. I made other plans for tonight."

He frowned. "Just what am I supposed to do tonight?"

She shrugged. "Have dinner with your parents. They're always asking you."

"Family dinner is tomorrow night as you very well know."

"So? Make it two nights. Your mother will love it." Did Dale hear the hint of bitterness in her voice? Often he'd cancelled dates with her to do something for his mother, and it had been a sore spot for Molly.

"But I want to be with you tonight, Molly. I was counting on it." His mouth drooped and he touched her arm. "Please, change your plans. I miss you."

Her heart melted and she smiled. "Do you really?"

"Of course!"

She leaned close and kissed him and he jerked back, red with embarrassment. She shook her head and sighed heavily. "I really can't change my plans, Dale. It's business. Business must come first today." She touched a piece of pewter. "In fact, I must go away on business for a while. I don't know when I'll be back. I'll try to make it soon."

"Where are you going?"

"I can't talk about it now."

He squared his shoulders. "Molly, how can you do this now of all times? You know I wanted to talk about our future, about our marriage."

She stiffened. She never realized until now that he always used that line when he wanted his own way. "We'll talk when I get back."

He stood stiffly, his eyes cold. "Very well, Molly. You'd better leave now and let me get back to work. Mr. Mathis will be here in a few minutes to discuss this department with me."

A shiver ran down Molly's back and she shot a look around. "Why didn't you tell me?"

Dale gripped her arm. "Don't you dare hang around and pounce on him for an interview."

"Don't worry. I won't."

"You won't?"

She shook her head and chuckled. "You can relax for today, Dale. I won't do anything more to embarrass you. But one of these days you'll be proud that I'm the reporter of the *Freburg News*. Wait and see."

He stabbed his fingers through his thick blond hair. "What are you up to, Molly? I don't like the look in your eye. What're you planning?"

She tapped his arm and laughed. "Don't you worry, Dale. I'll call you."

"Tonight?"

"I'll try. Bye." She leaned forward. "I love you."

"I love you." He looked around, then kissed her a quick, hard kiss. "Now, go before Mr. Mathis sees us."

Butterflies fluttered in her stomach at the thought and she rushed to the elevator that would take her to the main floor. Just as she stepped into one elevator Quinn Mathis stepped out of another. Perspiration popped out above her lip and she ducked her head and pressed the button, then faced the wall inside the elevator. Thankfully the doors slid shut. Weakly she leaned against the shiny bar until strength surged back into her legs.

Several minutes later she walked to the parking lot and slid into her yellow Mustang. She tossed the bag that held her other clothes to the back seat. Her blouse clung to her damp skin and strands of hair stuck to her wet face and neck. Suddenly the realization of what she'd done pressed in on her and she moaned. She wasn't the type of person who would deceive others, yet that was exactly what she'd done to Quinn Mathis. She pressed her lips tightly together. "I don't care! I must get that story!"

With a trembling hand she pulled Quinn's card from her purse even though she already knew where his estate was. All the homes on Oregon Avenue were gigantic and beautiful. Soon she would be living there. She could get her story and be on her way.

She frowned. What about her promise to stay six months? "Too bad," she said airily.

She turned the ignition and the car sputtered. "You're getting too old, car. Now start, and don't give me any grief." She tried again and it started reluctantly. She would take it to the garage for Jack to check before she dared drive to the country.

At the garage she watched as Jack looked under the hood and shook his head. Another mechanic whistled as he worked at a car on a hoist.

Jack turned to Molly. "I don't know, Molly. I think you'd better leave it here and let me check out the bendix. You need a new air filter I see."

"I can't leave it now, Jack. I need it."

He pushed his greasy cap to the back of his damp brown hair. "You can use my pickup if that'd help."

"Great idea! But I need my car by tonight, Jack."

"I'll do my best."

"Thanks." Molly smiled. "How's Tina?"

"Just fine. We're sure proud of our tiny son." Jack narrowed his dark eyes and studied Molly thoughtfully. "Just when are you going to get around to getting married? You and me are the same age and I already have a wife and baby. I always thought a beautiful girl like you would beat me to the altar."

Molly laughed. "Marriage isn't everything, Jack, but I'm working on it."

"Keep it up." He looked at her closely and tapped a wrench in the palm of his hand. "You look different. Your clothes, I guess. Are you in disguise or something?"

"Or something," she answered with a breezy laugh. Trust Jack to notice the difference in her appearance.

"What story are you working on now?"

"It's undercover."

"And you can't even tell your old friend Jack?"

"Nope!" She glanced around. "Where's your pickup? I've got to go." Jack wouldn't like what she was doing either. He had high standards.

"Here's the key." He dropped it in her hand. "The red pickup next to the tire rack is mine. If you're not here at closing, I'll take your car to my place and you can pick it up there."

"Sure thing, Jack. Thanks. See you later."

"Come for supper next week, why don't you? Tina would love seeing you again. And we want to show off the baby." Jack hesitated. "Bring Dale if you want."

Molly nodded, and walked to the pickup. Dale didn't like Jack because his hands were always dirty. Jack knew how Dale felt and stayed clear of him as much as possible. They saw each other often since they attended the same church, but never had much to say to each other. Molly pressed her lips tightly together as she drove down Pine Street. One of these days she'd tell Dale what a snob he was being about Jack.

She stopped at a red and white stop sign, then stared in surprise. Just where was she going?

"Molly, what are you up to?" She knew the answer to that. She was a block away from Oregon Avenue, and only a few minutes' drive away from the Mathis estate. She slipped on the tinted glasses, pinned her hair back in a knot and buttoned her blouse to her chin. "You're Molly Lynn from now on, my girl," she whispered.

Her skin pricked with excitement as she drove down Oregon Avenue. A black Chevy passed her and disappeared over a hill. Large oaks and maples lined the paved road. A tall black horse stood with its head over a white board fence while a herd of horses grazed in the green field. Fluffy white clouds dotted the bright blue sky. The sun shone almost directly over a grove of poplars. She slowed at the Mathis estate driveway. The pickup coughed and sputtered, then died. "Oh, no! I forgot to down-shift." Frantically she turned the key and pressed the gas. The pickup started and she let her breath out in relief. She certainly didn't want to be caught snooping around here now.

A dog barked and birds sang in the tall leafy trees. A small blue car drove past and Molly turned her head away just in case someone would recognize her.

At the stop sign a black and gray Cadillac slowed, then turned in beside her. The driver looked up just as she looked down. Her eyes locked with Quinn Mathis's. Her face flamed and she wanted to sink out of sight.

She watched Quinn stop and start to back up. Frantically she pushed the glasses up on her nose and wiped the lip gloss off with a tissue.

He rolled down his window and music drifted up to Molly. "We meet again, Molly."

She nodded, unable to speak.

"Would you mind coming to meet the girls now

since you're this close to my place?"

She hesitated.

"It would be more convenient for me, Molly. I've a business appointment in Madison early in the morning and I have to fly out tonight. I was going to call you." He waited and finally she nodded in agreement.

"I'll turn around and follow you," she said as calmly as possible. She watched his window slide up as he drove away.

Blood pounded in her ears as she turned and slowly followed him down the tree-lined drive to a large house that looked like a gorgeous Southern mansion. She saw two barns and a smaller house through the trees. Flowers of all colors and sizes grew in large beds throughout the lush green lawn.

She parked beside Quinn, clutched her purse and opened the pickup door. Before she could drop to the ground he caught her arm and helped her to the paved drive. His touch burned her skin and she pulled away, irritated at her reaction to him.

"Your place is beautiful, Mr. Mathis."

"Thank you. It's been in the family for years." He had pulled off his tie and unbuttoned his shirt at the throat. She pulled her gaze away from the strong brown column of his neck and looked toward the house again.

"Shall we go meet the girls, Molly?"

"Yes, but I can't stay now."

"You can come back later."

She nodded and walked beside him along the wide sidewalk to the side door.

Chapter 3

Molly's feet sank into the rust-colored carpet of the door-lined hallway. Quinn walked beside her, deep in thought. She smelled bayberry candles and a hint of Quinn's aftershave. She glanced at the grouping of watercolors on the wall that accented the earth-tone colors of the hall. As they passed an open door Molly glanced in and saw a uniformed woman with brilliant red hair setting a flower arrangement on the table. Molly's eyes widened in alarm and she stumbled slightly. It was Amber Ainslie! Amber Ainslie, Private Detective! Why was she working here? Was she here on assignment? Molly bit back a groan. Would Amber give her away?

Molly's heart sank and for one wild minute she thought of turning to Quinn and telling him the truth. Abruptly she pushed the thought aside. Somehow she'd get to Amber and try to explain what she was doing, and why. Amber surely wouldn't stop her from getting her story, would she? They were best friends in high school, but had drifted apart when they attended different colleges.

Quinn touched Molly's back, guiding her into a large family room. His touch tingled through her and she moved slightly to get away from the feel of his hand.

"Hello, Mom," he said crossing the room to kiss

the ash blond woman sitting on a long flowered sofa. She wore a yellow blouse with a white suit that showed off her good figure.

"Hello, Quinn." She smiled at him, then studied Molly with alert brown eyes.

Molly wanted to run from the steady gaze, but she stood beside the couch and waited. Mrs. Mathis had seen her several times. If she was recognized it would all be over. But Mrs. Mathis smiled and greeted her and Molly breathed easier.

The two girls at the wide window turned slowly and Molly saw tears on their pale cheeks. Immediately they brushed them away and walked toward their uncle. "Hello, Uncle Quinn," they said in one voice.

"Hello, girls." He bent to them and kissed their cheeks.

Tears burned the backs of Molly's eyes. Oh, what was she doing? Could she actually take advantage of their terrible situation just to get a story?

Quinn stood with an arm around each girl as he said, "Mom, girls, this is Molly Lynn. She's here to take care of you girls. Molly, this is my mother, Willa Mathis, and my two nieces, Deanie and Tonya."

Mrs. Mathis stood and gripped Molly's hand in a firm shake. "I'm glad Quinn hired you, my dear. I know you'll manage very well."

Molly forced back her guilt feelings. "Thank you. I'll do my best."

"I'm sure you will."

The girls stood close to Quinn, studying Molly with wide, dark eyes. Deanie had long, dark red hair that hung down her thin back. She rubbed her hands down her yellow shorts and softly said, "Hello."

Tonya was older and taller than Deanie. Her long dark hair was pulled away from her small face and held back with two pink barrettes that matched her sunsuit. She didn't speak or smile.

"I'm glad to meet both of you girls," said Molly with a gentle smile. "We'll have fun together, I'm sure."

I told Jane to get the yellow bedroom ready for you," said Mrs. Mathis. "It's just across the hall from the girls and down from me."

"That's fine, Mrs. Mathis," said Molly.

"Who is Jane, Mom?" asked Quinn.

"I hired her today. Bella had to take a couple weeks off to be with her sick mother."

"Did I just see her in the small dining room? Red hair, freckles?"

Molly held her breath.

Mrs. Mathis nodded. "Jane Kearny. Very capable."

Molly glanced toward the door. Amber *was* here undercover! She was calling herself Jane Kearny! But why? Was she investigating Steve's death?

"Molly, I'll have Jane show you to your room now," said Quinn.

"No!" Molly backed away. "Wait, please. I really don't . . . don't have time."

"But we'll be gone when you come tonight." He studied her with his fine brows cocked questioningly.

She managed to look up and meet his gaze. "The girls will be here. And Jane . . . will be. If you don't mind, I'd rather go now and see my room later." She edged toward the door as she talked. "I really must hurry now. It was nice meeting you, Mrs. Mathis, and you too, girls."

Quinn reached out and gripped her arm and she was forced to stop. "I'll walk you to your car." He looked over his shoulder to his mother. "I'll be right back."

Molly held her breath as they walked down the hall past the dining room. What if Amber saw her? Shivers ran down her spine.

"Are you all right, Molly?"

"Yes. Fine."

"You're trembling."

She glanced up at him to find a thoughtful expression on his face. "I'm excited about working here, I suppose."

He opened the door and she stepped out into the bright sunlight. "We didn't talk about a day off for you, Molly. Would Sundays be all right?"

"Yes." That would give her a chance to see Dale.

Quinn stopped beside the pickup. "The girls can't take another upheaval in their lives at this time. Are you sure that you can stay the full six months?"

Her throat closed over and all she could do was nod.

"In six months my sister and her husband will be back from Europe and they'll take the girls. Jan and Neville are the legal guardians, but they can't come home until then. It would be too hard on the girls to have a succession of nannies. You can understand that, can't you?"

Could he feel her hesitation? Maybe he could tell that she'd be long gone before six months, hopefully before six days.

"Molly, it's not too late to back out."

"No! No, please, I want the job."

"Fine. I'll see you when I get back from Madison. If you have any questions or need any help, talk to Jane. If Mom trusts her, then so do I. I'm sure Jane will help you get settled in."

"Yes, I'm sure." Molly reached to open the pickup door just as Quinn did. Her hand touched his and sparks shot to her heart. She jerked her hand back and he frowned slightly.

"You're too tense, Molly. I know you're shy, but think of us as family and try to relax."

"I will."

He opened the door and helped her inside, and she managed a smile as he closed the door. He stood beside the pickup with his hands resting lightly on his lean hips and his feet apart. "I am trusting you with the girls, Molly. I know you won't let me down."

She swallowed hard and managed another smile. Her hand trembled as she turned the ignition key and started the pickup. As she drove away she saw him finally walk back to the house. At the end of the drive she wiped her damp face with a tissue and leaned back with a ragged sigh. "Molly, Molly, what have you done?"

The tight collar of her blouse seemed to choke her and she unbuttoned it and rubbed her throat. Hot wind blew through the window and she rolled it up and turned on the air. She dare not think about Quinn and the girls and the promise that she knew she would break.

Right now she had to go home and pack, write a letter to her parents, and pick up her car. Hopefully, Mom and Dad would stay in Arizona until her job was finished. They wouldn't approve of her deception. Writing to them without telling them what she was working on would be hard. Usually she told them everything about her work, and they were always proud, but this time she couldn't tell them anything.

At the garage Jack handed her the car keys. "It's ready to go, Molly. But it does need more work, so as soon as you can leave it a few days, bring it back."

"Thanks, Jack." She paid him then said, "Have

you seen much of Amber Ainslie lately?"

He nodded. "She and Tina had lunch last week. She's looking for a country home. Says she wants to get out of the place where she lives now."

"I suppose she's busy working on a case."

"She said she had an undercover job to do for a while. But she couldn't talk about it, naturally."

"It's been a while since I've visited with her."

"You two were always together in school."

Molly nodded. "We were great friends." Would Amber remember that when she showed up tonight as Molly Lynn instead of Molly DuPree?

At seven o'clock Molly rang the doorbell of the Mathis home and waited with her bags beside her. Her legs felt as if she'd run for five miles. Her mouth felt bone dry.

She glanced toward the garage where her yellow Mustang was parked in the spot Quinn had assigned her. She breathed deeply. The evening air was pleasantly cool and scented with the aroma of fresh-mown grass. She touched the waist of her black slacks and made sure her gray blouse was tucked in. She had left off all makeup, not even bothering with the makeup to make her look pale and lifeless since she knew Quinn and his mother would be gone. Her mass of light brown curls was once again pulled severely back from her face and pinned in a knot at the nape of her neck. Without eye makeup, lip gloss or blush she felt exposed and plain. She certainly wasn't Dad's brilliant butterfly now. Maybe Amber wouldn't recognize her. She smiled and rang the doorbell again.

Finally the door opened and Amber stood there with a dishtowel in her hands. "Yes?" Her eyes widened as she held out a trembling hand. "Molly? Are you the Molly Lynn that I'm expecting?"

"Yes."

"Oh, no! But why?"

"I can explain, Amber. Please, give me a chance, and don't do or say anything to give me away to the family." Molly set her bags inside and closed the door.

Amber rubbed her hands down her skirt. How was she going to get around this situation? "I can't believe my own eyes. Is it really you? You didn't give up your writing, did you?"

"I'll tell you everything later in privacy. Where are the girls? Are Mr. Mathis and his mother gone?"

Amber nodded. "They left on time and won't be back until tomorrow or Wednesday." Amber picked up a case while Molly grabbed the other one. "I'll take you to your room and then get the girls. They're with Barney now. He's the handyman here and he's building a doghouse for their dog. I told Barney we'd come get the girls after you're settled in."

Molly fell into step beside Amber. "Barney? Do I know him?"

"Barney Meade. He's been with Steve Mathis for almost eight years."

Molly gripped her case tighter. "I know you're a detective, Amber."

Amber rubbed a spot on the bannister. "I thought so."

"Well?"

"Well what?"

"They call you Jane. Mrs. Mathis said she hired you today."

Amber nodded. She wanted to tell Molly everything, but she couldn't.

Molly moved restlessly. "Are you going to give me away?"

"Will you give me away?"

"Who hired you and why?"

"You know I can't answer either question."

Molly sighed heavily. "I know."

"And why are you here?"

Molly leaned against the railing. "To get a story."

"I see."

"Will you keep my secret?"

"I don't want to, but I will. We'd better hurry." Amber led the way to the yellow room and set Molly's bag inside. "This is it, Molly."

"It's beautiful! I love yellow and brown and greens together! And it's so big! My own desk and table and sofa."

"It's not your ordinary bedroom, is it?" Amber laughed, her cheeks flushed. "Wait'll you see my rooms."

"Wouldn't it be grand to own a home like this, Amber?"

"I'll say!" Amber rested her hands on her waist. She'd been looking for just the right country home, but this was way out of her price range. "I thought you'd be married by now, Molly."

"Me, too. I was too busy getting my career underway, and now Dale and I want to save money enough to get a good start before we get married."

"Dale? Do I know him?"

"Dale Gerard. He works at Ardetts. Blond, nice-looking man about thirty."

"What does he think of you working here as the great Lois Lane?"

"Well . . ." Molly grinned as she sat at the corner of the sofa. She picked up a pillow and hugged it to her. "He doesn't know."

Amber dropped to the edge of a chair and locked her hands around her knees. "Molly, Molly. What an adventure! You and I together again. Just like when we were in school!"

"Not quite," said Molly with a laugh. She propped the pillow in the corner of the sofa and leaned forward. "Can I really trust you?"

"Yes." Amber saw the serious look in Molly's blue eyes. "On my word of honor as a Christian."

Quickly she told Amber how and why she had taken the job. "I need an interview with him, Amber, and I can't leave until I have one."

"Oh, Molly, the girls. What are you doing to the little girls?"

Molly flushed painfully. "I'm sorry about that."

"Sorry doesn't do it, does it, Molly?"

"I'll think of some way to make it up to them. I promise!"

"I don't know how you think you'll get information from Quinn Mathis. He's a very private person. He hates for anyone to pry into the accident." Amber hesitated. She wanted to find out if Molly knew more than she was letting on. "And he gets very upset if anyone asks why he took over Ardetts instead of Mark Petersen."

Molly's brows shot up. "What have you learned about it, Amber? Is that why you're here? I didn't hear anything about Mark Petersen being in line for Steve's job."

Amber knew Molly was telling the truth. "I can't tell you anything. I did promise to be discreet about the Mathis's private business."

Molly bounded up and stood over Amber. "But this is different, Amber! I need to know everything about this case. I want to get to the bottom of the deaths of Steve and his wife."

"They don't need more publicity."

Molly strode to the dresser and back again. "Tell me about the accident at least. Was it an accident?

Or did someone deliberately kill them?"

Amber sat very still. "Is that possible? Is that what Mr. Mathis is thinking? It would certainly explain his actions. Maybe someone tampered with the brakes. Could that be why the car wouldn't stop?"

Molly sucked in air. "I never heard anything about faulty brakes. I must learn the whole truth, Amber!"

"I'd like to know it too, Molly." She jumped up and tugged her skirt in place. "Let's get the girls and put them to bed, then we'll talk."

"Great!"

Amber stopped in the doorway and turned to face Molly. "I wish you would stay with the girls the full six months even if you get the story. You've always been good with kids."

Molly shrugged. "I'll think of something, Amber. I don't want the girls to suffer either."

"I believe you, but I don't think Quinn Mathis will." Amber walked beside Molly down the stairs, her hand on the smooth railing. "He's great with the girls, and they love him. They love Barney, too."

Molly stopped in the kitchen beside the baker's rack. "Do you think Quinn Mathis will stay here even after his sister takes the girls?"

"This estate belongs to him. I heard him talking about showing a woman around the place. I think he was talking about his future wife." Amber wrinkled her nose as if she'd smelled something rotten.

"Is he engaged?" Molly's heart jerked a strange little twitch.

"He's talking about it, I think. The woman's name is Yvonne something or other and his mother doesn't like her because she's been divorced. From things I've heard about her I don't like her either."

Molly leaned weakly against the mapleboard island. "Is it Yvonne Stoddard?"

"Yes! That's her name. Do you know her?"

Molly nodded grimly. "And so do you. Her name was Yvonne Graham."

Amber yelped and shook her head in disbelief. "I can't believe it! Quinn Mathis would never fall for Yvonne Graham. Why, I can remember every dirty trick she played on us in school. She had to be the best in everything, and she didn't care if she cheated to do it."

"Does she come here often?"

"Don't you know, Molly? She lives just down the road. Her husband gave her a fortune as a settlement and she bought the estate next door last month."

"I didn't know." Molly shook her head, her face suddenly gray. "I am doomed, Amber. If she sees me here, she'll make trouble for me. She would have the story printed on the front page of both papers in town. What am I going to do now?"

"Get the story and run before she sees you."

"It's not that easy, Amber."

"Since when did that stop the great Molly DuPree?"

Molly smiled weakly. "I don't feel so great right now, Amber." Molly flung her arm out and lifted her chin high. "Oh, what a tangled web we weave when first we practice to deceive!"

Amber laughed and nodded. "Ain't it the truth?"

"There's only one thing for me to do, Amber."

"Leave now?"

"No! I'll stay out of Yvonne's way. Somehow or other, I'll stay out of her way. And I'll work overtime to get my story so I can get out of here. What about you?"

"I keep a low profile. She hasn't lived around here since high school so she won't know that I'm a detective. Besides, I look a lot different than I did in school. She probably wouldn't recognize me. She'll think I'm Jane Kearny."

"She knows me."

"Your work puts you in the spotlight more than mine does," said Amber. "My name might be known, but not my face." She folded a dishtowel that someone had dropped on the counter beside the sink. "I'll get the girls."

"Why don't you relax and have a Coke?"

"Thanks. I will." Molly watched Amber walk out the door. The hum of the refrigerator sounded loud in the sudden silence. From somewhere outdoors a dog barked and a horse neighed. Molly reached for the Coke and poured it into a glass, her hand trembling slightly. She had sounded sure when she told Amber that she would stay out of Yvonne's way, but it wouldn't be that simple.

"I'll have to tell Quinn Mathis the truth." She groaned at the thought. If she didn't, she knew Yvonne would do so just for the pleasure of seeing her embarrassed. Yvonne was the type of person who would hold a grudge forever, and also would take revenge on anyone who had angered her. Molly had angered her often as well as made her jealous. Last week Molly had seen Yvonne downtown shopping and Yvonne had made fun of the way she was dressed, the car she drove, and the fact that she had to work for a living. Yvonne could afford to spend a fortune on clothes and she drove a small gold Mercedes. Her dark hair was now dyed blond to show off her wide brown eyes.

"You will never amount to anything, Molly," Yvonne had said.

Molly had squared her shoulders and lifted her chin. She'd looked Yvonne in the eye and without saying a word, had angered her until she sputtered with rage.

Molly sighed and rubbed the condensation off the outside of her glass. "Yvonne will love to expose me to Quinn Mathis if she can. What have I gotten myself into this time?"

The back door opened and the girls walked in with Amber. "We're here," said Amber brightly. "Girls, say hello to Molly."

"Hello," they said in tiny voices.

"Hello, Deanie. Hello, Tonya. Would you like apple slices before we go upstairs?"

"I'm not hungry," said Tonya.

"We can't eat when we're sad," said Deanie.

Molly's muscles tightened. Was getting a story worth the pain she might cause the girls? It was too late to think about that now. She forced a smile and held out her hands. "Let's go upstairs and get ready for bed."

Amber stood beside the kitchen table and watched them walk out. She flipped her long red hair over her slender shoulder and narrowed her eyes. "Evidently Molly doesn't know about the money Steve Quinn was accused of taking from Ardetts. I must work fast to solve my case before Molly spreads her story all over the paper."

Chapter 4

Amber held the telephone receiver to her ear and tapped her foot as she glanced around the kitchen. What was taking Mina so long to answer? She said she'd be home tonight. "Come on, Mina Streebe. Answer your phone. Or are you snooping around in my place again?"

With an impatient sigh, Amber started to drop the receiver in place when she heard Mina's breathless voice. Amber sagged in relief against the counter. Mina was always looking for trouble and she surely could find it. "You sound like you've been running."

"I was outdoors and I ran in to answer the phone." Mina sank to her chair and fanned her round, red face with a paper that had been lying beside the phone. Her loose-fitting flowered blouse hung down over her bright blue slacks. She kicked off her red and blue sandals. "I'll catch my breath in a minute. Did you learn anything yet?"

"No. How about you?"

"I did a credit check on both Steve and Barb and came up with zilch. But I did drive out to that house on Clinton Street."

"And?"

"It's not what you want. Too small and too old."

"How small is too small?"

"There's not enough room for me as well as you."

With a chuckle Amber hoisted herself onto the counter. She smoothed her skirt over her knees and crossed her ankles. Mina was her snoopy landlady Amber had hired to work for her just a few weeks ago. That decision was based on keeping Mina out of her hair more than anything else. But Mina did know everything about everything and she was a great help. Since her husband had died and her four grown children had moved to different states, she'd taken classes from karate to basket weaving, from psychology to the study of worms. But her greatest desire was to be another James Bond. She was short and plump and didn't know a thing about dressing with taste.

"Just what makes you think you're going to move in with me?"

Mina grinned and pushed her dyed red curls back. "Who would cook and clean for you if I wasn't around?"

"I'm doing it here. I'd do it myself."

"But you've gotten used to my doing it these past few weeks."

"You're right. So, you could drive to my place and do it. You don't have to live in."

"Who would answer all the questions you need answers to?"

Amber laughed. "I got along without you for a long time, Mina."

"Back to the other." Mina knew when to leave things alone. "I did hear a rumor that Steve was seeing another woman."

"What?"

"Don't shout."

"Sorry. What woman?"

"I haven't found out yet, but I will."

"I'm sure you will. Get any details you can."

Amber held the receiver tightly. "Have you heard talk that Steve was murdered?"

"A little. And I've got my own suspicions."

"Such as?"

"I'm going on the premise that Steve did not steal the money from Ardetts."

"Yes?"

"And if he didn't, someone did and framed Steve. That someone could've tampered with the brakes. We heard that the brakes didn't work and that's why the car crashed. So, it could've been murder."

"Well." Amber narrowed her eyes and twisted the phone cord. "That puts a new light on my investigation, doesn't it?"

"You already suspected it was foul play anyway, Amber Ainslie, so don't try to fool me."

Amber grinned. "I just didn't want to admit it out loud, that's all. For Mrs. Mathis's sake. She can barely face the fact that he's dead. Murder would just about do her in."

"Hiding your head in the sand doesn't change facts, Amber."

"I know. Talk to you tomorrow, Mina."

"I have an appointment to look at a house. It's closer to Freburg than you wanted, but it sounds great."

"Let me know. If it's something I'd like I'll take time to look at it." She had been looking for just the right country home since she received her inheritance from Grandma Ainslie.

"Another thing, Amber."

Amber stiffened at the sound of Mina's voice. "Yes."

"Fritz Javor called."

"What did the good sheriff of Bradsville want?"

"A dinner date with you. I told him you were on

a case."

"Mina, it's my business if I want to have dinner with Fritz."

"He's a womanizer, Amber, and you know it. But then that's why you feel safe in going out with him. In your heart you know you won't fall in love with him."

"Drop it, Mina."

"Sure. You don't want to hear the truth. You can't carry the hurt in your heart forever. So, your parents divorced. It happens. You can't let it keep you from loving and marrying."

"Goodbye, Mina."

"You listen to me, Amber Ainslie!"

"Call me when you have something important to tell me." Amber's hand shook as she hung the receiver in place. "Mind your own business, Mina," she whispered hoarsely.

A few minutes later Amber glanced toward the stairs, then slipped into Steve Mathis's study. While Molly was busy with the girls she'd go through Steve's papers. When Mrs. Mathis had hired Amber, she said there was nothing in Steve's study that could prove or disprove that he'd taken the money from Ardetts. Amber wanted to see if she could find something Mrs. Mathis may have overlooked.

Had Steve and Barb been murdered? If so, why?

Amber glanced around the study. It was nice. Wide glass doors leading to the patio let in the evening light. Maybe in her new home she could have a study with a stone fireplace like this one. She touched the burgundy leather sofa and matching footstool, then walked to the huge mahogany desk with inlaid leather top. She reached to the back of the top drawer where Mrs. Mathis had left the keys to the other drawers and the file cabinet. The keys jangled as she picked them up.

"I don't want my son's name ruined," Mrs. Mathis had said when she was in Amber's office several days ago. "He's suspected of taking fifty thousand dollars from the company. Steve wouldn't do that, but it looks like he has. I want you to learn the truth."

"No matter what it is?"

"No matter what."

"No matter what," muttered Amber as she unlocked the first desk drawer on the left. She pulled out a ledger and glanced through it. It was Steve's personal ledger, not from Ardetts. At a quick glance she couldn't see anything unusual. Steve had been very meticulous.

"I'd hate to pay their electric bill," muttered Amber as she dropped the book back in place. She glanced quickly over the contents of every drawer.

She turned to the huge mahogany bookcase on the wall opposite the fireplace. The top of the bookcase was open shelves and doors closed off the bottom. She opened the doors and looked at the shelves. After closer inspection she saw that the shelves on the right were narrower than the ones on the left. "I wonder."

She knelt down, the sand-beige carpet soft against her legs. Slowly, she ran her fingers over and around the shelves. She sat back and frowned thoughtfully, then rubbed her hand over the end of the shelves. She felt a slight indentation. "Well, well." Looking closer, she pressed the indentation. The shelves swung out like a thick door, revealing another door with no knob, but a keyhole. She grabbed the ring of keys, but none were small enough to fit.

"Who knows about this hidden door?" she asked just above a whisper. If Mrs. Mathis had known, she would have mentioned it. She had told Amber the combination to the safe which was behind the picture by the fireplace. Amber glanced up at the picture. It was a portrait of a big man sitting beside an antique table. It was done in oils in great detail, down to the objects on the table and the jade ring on the man's hand. Amber knew it was the first place she would look if she didn't know where the wall safe was hidden. It looked like a picture that would hide secrets.

Slowly Amber pushed the door closed and once again it looked like ordinary shelves. It would take a pro to spot the hidden door.

She ran to the huge picture that covered the safe and swung it out. Quickly she dialed the combination and opened the safe. It held a few dollars in cash, jewelry, some important documents, but no key, not even hidden in the jewel box. But the jade ring was there. She held it up to compare it with the ring on the man's finger. The painted ring was the exact size of the real ring. She touched the painted ring, then chuckled at the thought of slipping it off the man's finger. "It looks real enough," she said as she pushed the real jade ring back into its slot in the jewelry box.

Quickly she glanced through the documents, but found nothing that would help the case. A copy of their will showed that Steve and Barb had left everything to their children. Quinn was executor of the will and Jan and Neville Butler were the girls' guardians.

Amber stepped back and shook her head. Her fiery red hair bobbed over her slender shoulders and down her back.

"Where is that key?"

She had looked through the things that Steve had

in his pocket when he died. The only keys he carried were to his car, his office and his house.

Slowly she closed the safe and swung the picture in place. She wrinkled her nose at the stern-faced man, then turned to glance through the glass door. A movement caught her eye and she ducked to the side of the door and peeked out. Was someone hiding behind the huge maple?

A shiver ran down her spine. Maybe it was Barney. But he wouldn't be skulking around.

Amber hooked her bright red hair over her ears and narrowed her blue eyes as she tried to make out what looked like a figure. Maybe it was a dog. "Or my imagination," she muttered.

She dropped to the floor and crawled through the doorway into the hall. She leaped up and ran to the back door. Cautiously she opened the door and eased out, closing it quietly.

Soft, warm wind blew the scent of freshly cut grass to her. Crickets chirruped and a bird twittered. Shadows lengthened and she knew it would be dark before long. Barney's pickup was no longer parked outside the long garage.

Amber trembled. Her gun was in her room off the kitchen. Barney was gone and Molly was upstairs with the girls.

Amber lifted her chin and took a deep breath, then sprinted to the nearest tree big enough to hide her. She gathered her skirt close to her legs and carefully peeked around the tree. Someone was hiding behind a tree outside Steve's study. It was already too dark to make out any details. How could she reach the person without spooking him?

Before she could move, the person stepped out and ran toward Steve's study. The man was dressed in jeans and a light jacket with a cap pulled low on his head. Amber waited and watched. He reached for the door handle but found it locked. He reached into his pocket, pulled out a key, unlocked the door, looked around and slipped inside.

"What do you know," muttered Amber. She ran to the back door and quietly slipped inside, then ran lightly down the hall to Steve's study. The door was ajar as she'd left it. A light bobbed and she knew the intruder had a flashlight. She caught a whiff of cologne.

Just then Tonya raced down the wide stairs shouting at the top of her voice, "Jane, Jane, don't let her put me to bed!"

Amber heard something crash in Steve's study. She shoved open the door just as the intruder ran out the glass door, leaving it wide open. A vase that had been on the mantle lay smashed on the brick hearth.

"Jane!" cried Tonya, hurling herself at Amber.

Amber caught Tonya to her, helplessly looking over her head at the disappearing figure. Warm wind blew a leaf onto the carpet.

"Why's that door open?" asked Tonya, frowning up at Amber.

"Let's close it," said Amber. She walked across the study and pushed the door shut, then locked it. A lot of good it would do, she thought grimly. She clicked on the desk lamp and pulled the curtains closed. Maybe that would keep the intruder out. She bent down to Tonya. Amber could smell Tonya's freshly shampooed hair. "Now, what's all the shouting about?"

"*She* thinks she can put me to bed, but I don't want her to. I want you to."

"But Molly's your nanny." Amber brushed a tear off Tonya's pale cheek. "It's her job to put you to bed."

"I don't care!" Tonya twisted the tail of her yellow cotton pajama top around her finger. "I want you."

Amber bit back an impatient sigh and nodded. "Let's go." She took Tonya's hand and walked upstairs with her. "What do you have against Molly? She's nice."

"She told us a lie," said Tonya.

Amber stopped short at the top of the carpeted steps. "What lie?"

"She said she'd stay with us, but she won't. I know she won't. As soon as she falls in love with Uncle Quinn he'll send her away and someone else will come."

"What makes you think she'll fall in love with him?"

"She said she thought he was handsome."

"He is handsome."

"I know."

Amber bit back a laugh. "You might like to know that Molly is in love with someone named Dale."

"She is?"

"Yes."

"Then maybe she didn't lie."

Amber didn't say anything. She felt like finding Molly and telling her to leave tonight and never return. It was going to be hard on the girls when they learned who she really was. Amber bit the inside of her lip. But, who was she to talk? She also was here under an assumed name.

Wasn't it different with her though? She was here to solve a case. Molly was here to get a story.

Amber handed Tonya over to Molly then slowly walked back downstairs. She peeked in Steve's study. It was as she'd left it. What was the intruder after? Was it whatever was behind the locked door? She swept up the broken glass. Where was the key to the hidden door? She wanted to stay and look, but knew it would have to wait until Molly was in bed. Molly must not learn anything from her.

She found the scotch tape, ripped off a piece and taped it across the crack between the glass doors. If it was loose when she checked again, she'd know someone had slipped in.

Quickly she clicked off the light and went to her room to change into comfortable jeans and a cool pink blouse.

Later in the den Amber turned to Molly and said, "Are you working on this story alone?"

Molly stood just inside the den, her hands at her narrow waist as she studied Amber. What a strange question for Amber to ask. "Yes. Why?"

Amber thought of the intruder. "I just wondered. I don't want another surprise."

"You're angry with me, aren't you? Even after all this time, I can still read you."

"I suppose I am angry." Maybe she was really angry at not catching the intruder rather than at Molly.

Molly sank to the couch. "I don't blame you at all, Amber. I'm angry at myself. When I decided to come here I thought it would be all right to walk out on the girls, but now I can see the harm it'll do to them."

Amber dropped to the carpet, leaned against the brocaded chair and pulled her knees to her chin. "So, leave. Now. Tonight."

"No. You know I can't. I'll have to stay."

Amber sighed. "I suppose so."

"But I will tell Quinn Mathis the truth as soon as I can."

"When will that be?"

Molly pushed back a strand of light brown hair.

"After I learn something about the accident. When I can find the nerve."

"He's pretty intimidating."

"Oh, Amber, I wish I wouldn't have started this. But it's too late now." Molly hugged a pillow to her. "I just want to get my story."

"Why is it so important to you?"

Tears pricked the back of Molly's eyes. "It could be a big boost to my career. I could learn the truth about Steve's and Barb's deaths. Oh, I don't know! Maybe it's because Dale doesn't respect me as a reporter."

Amber saw the look of pain on Molly's face and she remembered all the years they'd had of sharing secrets. "Maybe he's jealous because your job is a little more glamorous than his."

Molly brushed away a tear. "He's not like that." She lifted her chin a fraction. "Amber, I do want to get to the bottom of the accident. If it *was* an accident. I have this feeling. And you know how often my feelings were right in the past."

"I remember."

Molly leaned forward. "Amber, could we work together on this case? Could we? I'll help you and you help me."

Amber considered it for a second, then shook her head. "I don't want to hurt your feelings, Molly, but I can't take a chance on anything leaking to the press before I want it to."

Molly bit her bottom lip. "You don't really trust me, do you, Amber?"

"It's not just you, Molly. I guess it's hard for me to trust anyone."

"Are you sure it's not just me?"

Amber rested her chin on her knees. "Did you know Mom and Dad divorced?"

"No! I hadn't heard."

"He had an affair."

"Oh, Amber!"

"Mom was crushed. It took me a long time to forgive Dad but, with God's help, I finally did."

"Is your dad the reason you're not married?"

"Of course not!" Amber jumped up. "I just haven't found the right guy yet."

Molly watched Amber pace the room, but didn't say a word.

Finally Amber faced Molly again. "If you learn anything about the accident, will you tell me?"

Molly thought for a minute, then nodded.

Chapter 5

Molly squared her shoulders, lifted her chin and knocked on the half-open door with an icy fist. She had decided that she would tell Quinn the truth today. When he returned home this afternoon she lost her nerve, then missed her opportunity when Yvonne Stoddard had arrived. Molly quickly took the girls for a long hike, then Amber had fed them dinner in the kitchen.

"Come in, Molly." Quinn sounded tired and depressed. He had been home for two days and had no opportunity to talk with Molly alone until now.

Stepping inside Steve's dimly-lit study, she observed Quinn sitting on the leather chair with his head back and his stocking feet propped on the coffee table. Locking her hands behind her back, she said, "I'm sorry to be so late, but it took a while to settle the girls for the night."

He lifted his head. Even in the shadows she could see the tired lines around his eyes. "That's all right. Yvonne just left." He wanted her to leave sooner.

Molly bit back a knowing grin as she sat in the corner of the soft leather couch. She crossed her legs and smoothed her skirt over her knees. The antique clock on the fireplace mantle ticked softly. A night bird called. Molly sat quietly, waiting for Quinn to speak first. She'd take her cue from him. If there was an opening, she'd tell him the truth about herself. Maybe.

After several minutes of silence he said, "The girls like you, Molly."

"I like them, too."

"I didn't realize you were an outdoor person. I think that helped."

She flushed, glad he couldn't see in the dim light. "I do like to hike and ride horseback." And ski, both snow and water, and camp and fish and hunt. She liked music and could play the guitar and sing like a pro. She read avidly, enjoyed watching TV, and loved making new friends. But none of that side of her showed to Quinn.

"The girls need someone to spend time outdoors with them. I don't have the time and Mother never was one for sports." He dropped his feet to the carpeted floor and leaned forward. "I would like you and the girls to have dinner with me from now on."

Her heart zoomed to her feet. "Oh?"

"It's the only chance I have to see them each day."

"I see."

"I've asked Jane to serve dinner at six so it won't be too late for them." He tugged on his open collar. "The girls need that family togetherness."

"You're right, of course."

"You don't seem too happy about it. Is something wrong?"

She sat very still. "Not at all." Yvonne was the problem. "I suppose I'm just tired tonight."

"It has been a long day, hasn't it?

"You should be in bed, Mr. Mathis."

He nodded and stifled a yawn. "I am tired. It's taken me the last two days to get caught up at the store. I almost put off talking to you again tonight, but I wanted you to know that I appreciate what you've done for the girls. They're more relaxed now and they actually laugh again. You've done more for them these few days than I did the two months since ... since Steve ... died."

"I'm glad I could help."

"I'm glad I hired you."

A nerve jumped in her cheek.

"If you need anything for them, let me know. I'll give you an allowance for their clothes and vitamins and such."

"Thank you."

"Is there anything you wish to discuss with me? It might be a while before we have privacy again."

She opened her mouth to blurt out the truth about herself, then bit back the words. She had to get information from him first. Once he knew why she was here, he'd kick her out without revealing anything.

"Were you going to say something, Molly?"

She shrugged. "I know the girls miss their parents badly."

"I know. Hopefully none of the scandal will touch them."

Molly froze. "Scandal?"

"The ... accident."

"The accident?"

"I can't talk about it."

"I'm sure it's been as hard for you as for them."

He nodded.

"Moving from Madison must have been difficult for you."

He lifted a shoulder. "I left friends behind, but it's only an hour's flight away, so I'm not totally cut off from them. And the Madison store is in good hands."

"I heard that Mark Petersen had intended to take over Ardetts here in town. He must resent your being here."

Quinn rubbed his jaw and Molly heard the raspy sound of whiskers. "Mark Petersen wouldn't have been good at the job, and he is upset that he didn't get it, but he seems content to be second in command for now. Do you know him?"

"Slightly." She'd interviewed him twice about the accident and gotten nowhere.

"Have you lived in the area all your life?"

She tensed, then nodded slightly.

"Your name's not in the phone book." Before she could say anything he continued. "I assume it's unlisted."

She didn't comment. How could she tell him that it was listed under M. DuPree? A moth flew against the glass door and she watched it, knowing the frustration it felt for not getting where it wanted to go.

"It's better with a woman living alone to have an unlisted number. Mother feels much better with the new number here."

Very casually Molly asked, "Were unwanted calls coming in?"

"Yes. After Steve and Barb died. There are crazy people out there who love to prey on suffering people." Quinn rubbed the ankle that rested on his knee. "So much conjecture is going on as to the cause of the accident. Many people called Mother to tell it all to her."

"Could there be anything to the gossip?"

"No. I don't think so."

"Your brother was a wealthy man and he probably had his share of enemies."

"Well, yes, but I don't think they'd want to kill him. Or I would be dead too."

Molly nodded thoughtfully. "People do kill people. Could someone have killed your brother and his wife?"

Quinn moved restlessly. "I don't think so."

"Are the police investigating?"

"No."

She leaned forward slightly. Had he hired Amber Ainslie? "Did you come here to investigate yourself?"

He nodded. "I want it settled once and for all. But that's a secret, Molly."

"Of course."

"I shouldn't have mentioned it, but it's very easy to talk to you."

"Thank you."

"I think I can talk to you, Molly, without fear of what I say being repeated outside this room."

A band tightened around her heart.

He sighed heavily. "I've also asked for an audit of the books at Ardetts." Abruptly he pushed himself up. "Forget I said that. I must be very tired to let that slip."

An audit! Well, well. Did Amber know? "Don't worry, Mr. Mathis. Your secret is safe with me." The words burned and she ducked her head to hide her lie. Soon she'd tell George Bailer everything and it would make headlines.

Quinn smiled. "Molly, I'm thankful I found you."

She flushed again, and couldn't meet his eyes. "Thank you."

He walked to the sound system built into the wall beside the fireplace. "Do you like music?"

"Very much."

He pushed a button and soft violin music filled the room. "I like many different kinds of music, but this is soothing after a very long day." He walked to the glass door and looked out into the star-studded night, his hands resting lightly on his lean hips. The moth fluttered away.

Molly walked around the desk and stood studying his profile. What strong features he had! Her heart stirred and she frowned.

He turned his head and looked into her eyes and she felt a strange sensation tug at her heart. "Mother, Barney and Jane have only good things to say about you, Molly. I'm thankful you all get along so well."

"They're nice people."

"Have you ever married, Molly?"

"No. You?"

He shook his head. "You said you're planning to marry next year."

"I hope to." She locked her hands tightly behind her back. "Is there anyone special for you?" Like Yvonne?

"Not at this time. I was in love a couple of times, but nothing ever came of it. I've been too busy with business."

"Your mother would probably like to see you married with a couple of kids."

He smiled. "You're right about that. She says that God has a special woman for me if I'd just open my eyes and see her, and stop working so hard." He chuckled. "I tell Mother that if I ever find someone like *her*, I'll grab her and marry her immediately."

"What about the woman who was here today? Is she the one?"

"Yvonne?" He frowned as if the subject of Yvonne upset him.

"Does she come to dinner often?" Molly held her breath as she waited for an answer.

Quinn walked to his chair and perched on the arm. "She would like to, but I told her today that dinner was my time with the girls, and that I plan to have it that way."

"Did you . . . mention me to her?"

"I told her that you were here. She says she knows a lot of people in town, but wasn't familiar with your name."

"Oh?"

"Yvonne Stoddard is her name. Do you know her?"

"I believe I've read it in the paper a few times." Molly leaned back against the desk. "She's divorced, isn't she?"

He nodded. "Her husband was much too old for her. I feel sorry for her because of what she had to endure the past four years of her marriage."

Molly bit back a cry of disgust. "He certainly left her with plenty of money to console her."

"I take it you don't approve."

"You're right!"

"Of money or divorce?"

"Divorce! Marriage is for life!" Her voice rang with conviction and she saw his surprised look as she lowered her dark lashes and added very primly, "At least, that's what I believe."

"I do, too, Molly, but it's not always that cut and dried." He sounded depressed again and she wondered what had caused it.

"A person should be sure of the other person before getting married, Mr. Mathis."

"Call me Quinn."

"Quinn." She liked the sound of his name on her lips.

"Once again I agree, Molly, but people wear masks. If a person doesn't want someone to see beneath the mask, then it's impossible to do so."

The conversation had suddenly become more than Molly had expected. She thought of her own mask and she moved uneasily. "But love gives the freedom to lower the mask, don't you think?"

"It should."

"Were Steve and Barb still in love?"

Quinn stiffened and shot a look at Molly. "Don't ask about something that doesn't concern you, Molly."

"I'm sorry. You're right. But I did hear that Yvonne Stoddard was seen alone with Steve on more than one occasion."

Quinn lifted his square chin and his eyes darkened. "The subject is closed, Molly. I think it's time for you to get to bed. The girls get up early."

The chill in his voice alarmed her, but strengthened her resolve to get to the bottom of the mystery. Slowly she stood and faced him. "I wouldn't think you'd want to entertain a woman who caused friction in your brother's home."

"That will be all!"

She bowed her head to hide the flash of understanding in her eyes. So, he was seeing Yvonne to learn the truth! "I'm sorry if I upset you."

"Good night, Molly." His voice was brisk. "I'll see you at dinner tomorrow."

"Yes. At dinner." She walked to the door, then turned. "Good night, Mr. Mathis."

"Quinn. Remember?"

"Quinn."

He wearily rubbed a hand across his face. "I didn't mean to bark at you, but some things are touchy to me." He clicked off the music and slowly walked to the door. "Sleep well."

"Thank you. You, too. Try not to carry your worries to bed."

He smiled briefly. "I'll try. But it's not easy."

"Especially when there's such a mystery surrounding the death of your brother."

He nodded, and she walked away before he told her again to mind her own business. She climbed the stairs, her head spinning. Should she call George Bailer at home and tell him what Quinn had said? George expected her to check in with him regularly. She stopped at the top of the stairs and frowned. She would not call George until she had something concrete to tell him.

In her room she dropped her glasses on the dresser, slipped on cool shorts and a blouse, pulled the pins from her bun, brushed her hair until it curled and waved the way she liked it, then put on her pale blue sandals. She'd check the girls just to make sure they were sleeping soundly before she went to talk with Amber.

Just how much should she tell Amber?

Molly walked across the quiet hall and peeked into the bedroom the girls shared. Tonya slept soundly, her arms outside the cover, but Deanie whimpered and moaned, then sat bolt upright, her eyes wide with fear.

Molly ran to her before she cried out and woke Tonya. "Shhh. You're all right, Deanie. You're here and you're safe." Molly dropped to the edge of the bed and pulled Deanie onto her lap.

Deanie whimpered and curled against Molly, clinging to Molly's neck. "I'm not really scared, Molly. Honest."

"I'm glad you let me hold you. You're as cuddly as a teddy bear."

Deanie giggled and relaxed her tense body. "Don't tell Tonya. She might think I'm a big baby."

"We'll keep it our secret. Close your eyes now and go back to sleep." Molly hummed softly as she sat on the edge of the bed and rocked Deanie. After a few minutes she gently laid Deanie back in bed and pulled the cover up to her chin. "Sleep tight, honey."

"Don't leave yet."

"I won't."

"Will you pray for me so I'm not scared? That's what Mommie used to do."

Molly nodded. "Heavenly, Father, thank you for watching over Deanie as she sleeps. Help her to have a good night's rest so she can run and play tomorrow. We love you. In Jesus' Name, Amen."

"Amen," whispered Deanie.

"I'll sit here and rub your back for a while."

Deanie flipped to her stomach and Molly rubbed Deanie's back, humming as she did. After a while Deanie's breathing grew even and Molly bent and kissed her warm cheek. Molly turned to leave, then stopped short to find Quinn standing in the open doorway watching her. She looked quickly back at Deanie. Molly swallowed hard. She'd left her glasses in her room. Oh, what if he recognized her?

She glanced at him again to see him looking at her with a soft look in his eyes. Her heart leaped a funny little jerk as she pushed her hair back. He didn't move as she walked toward him. His shirt hung outside his pants, unbuttoned several buttons, and showing the fine hairs on his chest. "I didn't hear you," she said with a catch in her voice.

"I came to check the girls and saw you with Deanie, so I didn't disturb you." He stepped aside for Molly to walk into the dimly-lit hallway. "Did she have another nightmare?"

"I don't know. She was starting to sob in her sleep when I walked in."

"My room is in the other wing of the house and too far away to hear her. I'm thankful you're here."

His words pleased her out of all proportion to what he said and she smiled.

He studied her more closely. "You have beautiful hair, Molly."

She flushed and couldn't meet his eyes.

"You should never pin it in a bun."

"I . . . I don't . . . think we . . . should talk about my hair."

"You're right, of course." He suddenly seemed to notice his open shirt and buttoned it. "I think you'll be able to help Deanie. She's afraid that everyone she loves will die and leave her alone."

Molly finally managed to force words past her tight throat. "I'll do what I can for her."

"I know you will." Quinn rattled the change in his pockets. "Tonya can express her pain, but Deanie holds hers in. She has taken to you, Molly, and I'm thankful that you'll be here these six months while we're waiting for Jan."

Molly looked down at the carpet to hide the hot tears that burned the back of her eyes. "I'll do what I can," she said again.

"I know you will. You're a caring woman." He touched her slender shoulder and her head shot up. His eyes were warm and tender. "Good night, Molly. You didn't know it, but you helped me tonight, too."

"I did?" she whispered.

"Yes. Thank you."

"Any time."

"I needed someone to talk to and you were there, talking and listening. Mostly listening. I appreciate it."

A bitter taste filled her mouth and she nodded slightly. "Good night," she said in a low, tight voice.

"Good night."

She walked to her room and closed the door. Weakly she leaned against it, her hands pressed to her hot cheeks. "Dear God, what am I doing?"

She paced from the couch to the bed and then to the bathroom door. Oh, she couldn't face anyone tonight, not even Amber. Especially not Amber. Molly crept to her bed and after a long time, fell asleep.

The next evening, after a fun-filled day with the girls, Molly tiptoed to the dining room and peeked inside to make sure only four places were set for dinner. She'd changed from jeans to a soft blue dress that nipped in at her slender waist and flared out to below her knees. After a lot of thought she kept her hair in a bun and slipped her glasses on. She wanted to brush her hair to fluff around her face and down onto her shoulders and back. How she wanted Quinn to know that she wasn't plain! Her blue eyes flashed. What was she thinking? What Quinn Mathis thought of her looks wasn't important.

Just then the girls dashed from the study with Quinn right behind them. He smiled at Molly and said, "Hi."

"Hi," she said just above a whisper.

Amber carried in the food, hiding a frown as she glanced at Molly. Last night she expected Molly to report to her, but she hadn't come. Molly promised to meet her after the girls were in bed tonight.

"The chicken smells wonderful, Jane," said Quinn.

"The salad looks too beautiful to eat," said Molly.

"Then do I have to eat mine?" asked Deanie with a twinkle of mischief in her eye.

"Yes, you do, young lady," said Quinn sternly. He grinned and shook his finger at her. "You know you do."

"I like mashed potatoes, Jane," said Tonya. "You make them nice and fluffy and full of butter."

"I'm glad you like them," said Amber. She stood behind Deanie's chair as Quinn asked the blessing on the food, then she served the girls and walked back to the kitchen to eat.

"I can almost swim, Uncle Quinn," said Tonya. "Molly's teaching me."

"Good."

"I know I'm better than Tonya," said Deanie.

"No, you aren't," said Tonya.

"You are both doing very well," said Molly as she lifted a bite of tomato to her mouth.

"Will you be gone all day Sunday, Molly?" asked Quinn as he set his glass of water back in place.

She nodded. "Unless you need me."

"I can manage I think. I'm taking the girls on a picnic."

"A picnic!" the girls cried, clapping.

"We'll go after church Sunday if it doesn't rain," said Quinn.

Molly suddenly wanted to put aside her day with Dale and spend it with Quinn and the girls. The thought startled her and she could only pick at dessert.

As they walked to the family room later, she tried to forget the surprising thought that she'd rather be with Quinn and the girls Sunday than with Dale, but it persisted.

Quinn walked to the hearth and watched the girls clinging to Molly. There was something special about Molly and he realized that he wanted to know her better.

"Sing for us again, Molly," said Deanie. "Please."

Molly picked up her guitar that she'd stood in the corner earlier and strummed a few chords before she broke into a contemporary gospel song that she liked. She perched on the edge of a chair, her face glowing with happiness. Next she started singing "Bullfrogs and Butterflies" and to her surprise Quinn joined in when the girls did. His voice was a strong baritone that blended with her soprano. When the song ended, Quinn strode from the room. Disappointed, Molly looked after him.

"Sing another song, Molly," said Deanie, sitting cross-legged on the carpet at Molly's feet.

Molly plucked at the strings. "Are you sure you don't want to watch TV?"

"I don't," said Deanie, and Tonya echoed the same.

Molly sang "Fallin' in Love with You." To her surprise Quinn walked in with a guitar, singing and playing along with her. When the song ended he smiled at her and the smile zoomed straight to her heart. She looked away, blood pounding in her ears. He sat on the coffee table in front of her and played a song that she knew. She joined in, singing the harmony to his melody.

"I haven't enjoyed myself this much in a long time," he said with a smile that showed even, white teeth. "Do you sing professionally, Molly?"

"Just in church and special gatherings and things like that. I never did want to go big time with singing." Only with writing. The thought sent a sharp pain through her and she had to force herself to continue singing with Quinn.

Chapter 6

Saturday afternoon Molly sliced through the water, then swam to the shallow end where the girls played. Maybe tonight Quinn would open up enough to tell her all he knew about the accident. Each day he talked more freely to her.

"I want to learn to dive just like you," said Tonya as she clung to the ladder that led down into the pool. Her small body floated out from her arms. "Will you teach me?"

"I'll help you all I can."

"I want to learn too," said Deanie, bobbing up and down. "I can already swim. See?" She sank under the water, splashing her hands hard against the top of the water. "I know how to swim, but Tonya doesn't."

"I do too!" Tonya kicked the water hard, but didn't let go of the ladder.

Molly pushed herself to the tiled edge of the pool. Water ran off her onto the tile. She squeezed out the braid that hung down her back. The hot sun dried her back and arms immediately. "You're both doing very well."

Deanie climbed out of the pool and plopped down beside Molly. "Mommie was teaching us how to swim." Her voice broke and she ducked her head.

"Don't talk about Mommie," snapped Tonya. "She's dead and she's never coming back."

"She's not coming back to live here because she lives in heaven now," said Molly. "Only her body is dead. She's alive in heaven right now living where Jesus lives."

"That's right," said Deanie, moving closer to Molly. "Uncle Quinn said so."

"I bet she's lonely without us," said Tonya. She crept out of the pool and stood beside Molly.

Molly pulled Tonya close. "She knows your uncle loves you and is taking care of you," said Molly. "He'll be home after a while and he'll have lots of hugs and kisses for you."

"I love Uncle Quinn," said Deanie.

"Did I hear my name?"

Molly jerked around to see Quinn standing near a deck chair. He wore jeans and a white knit shirt with short sleeves, showing off his tan arms and face. "Hi," she whispered.

"Uncle Quinn!" the girls flew to him, dotting his clothes with water.

"I decided to come home a little early today to see my girls." Quinn kissed their cheeks, then looked over their heads at Molly.

Scooping up her towel and wrapping it around herself, she flushed, grabbed her glasses and slipped them on.

Later, just inside the back door Quinn stopped Molly with a light touch on her arm. She jumped as if she'd been burned and his brow shot up. "I'd like to see you in my study as soon as possible."

Her stomach tightened in fear. Had he learned her true identity? With a great deal of effort she forced her reply to sound normal. "I'll be down as soon as I help the girls change."

"Fine." He turned toward the study and Molly walked upstairs, gripping the bannister for support.

"I had fun today," said Tonya.

"Me too," said Deanie.

"So did I," said Molly as she helped the girls into the shower. She rinsed out the swimsuits, then leaned against the counter with her eyes closed. After her talk with Quinn, would she be booted out? Pushing the thought aside, she helped the girls dry off and change into jeans and tee shirts. As she caught a glimpse of her reflection in the large mirror over the sink, her eyes widened in alarm. She certainly didn't look like the pale, quiet woman that she'd presented to Quinn in his office the other day. She forced back her panic as she finished with Tonya and Deanie. "You girls may watch the Cinderella video in the family room while I change."

With glad shouts they ran downstairs while Molly walked to her room for a quick shower. She dressed in a simple tan shirtwaist, applied makeup to turn her skin sallow and slipped her feet into flats. Mercilessly she brushed her hair back until it lay flat on her head and pinned it in place at the nape of her neck. She pushed her glasses in place and said, "There. That's better."

Slowly she walked down the stairs. Smells of roast beef and coffee drifted from the kitchen. Sounds of Cinderella and the girls' laughter floated out from the family room. Molly took a deep breath as she stopped outside Steve's study. She lifted her trembling hand to knock, then stopped at the sound of voices inside. Quinn was talking with a woman. Yvonne? Molly sucked in her breath and backed away, then spun around and sped to the kitchen. She grabbed Amber's arm. "Who's in the study with Quinn?"

"I don't know. What's wrong?"

"It's a woman. I have a meeting with him but if it's Yvonne I can't waltz in there and ruin everything." Molly strode to the table and back again. "What am I going to do?"

Amber sighed heavily. "I suppose you want me to go in there?"

"Oh, would you?"

"I guess so."

"Amber, you saved my life!"

Amber chuckled. "I'll take an iced tea. But you owe me one."

"Anything! I mean it!"

"Give me all the information you haven't told me yet."

Molly sank to a kitchen chair with a slight nod. She still hadn't mentioned that Steve and Yvonne had been seen together. "I know I should've told you, but Yvonne was seen with Steve Mathis several times."

Amber lifted her brows. Mina had tried to learn who the other women in Steve's life was, but no one would say. "Oh? And is it true?"

"Yes."

"I hate to hear that! If a man would step out on his wife he might also take money from his own company." Amber lifted the jug of tea out of the refrigerator and plunked it on the counter. She dropped ice cubes into two glasses, then leaned close to Molly. "I hate this case, Molly! I pray that Steve really wasn't sneaking out on his wife or it'll break his mother's heart."

"I know."

"Is there anything else you haven't told me?"

"Quinn's going to have the books audited next week."

"I know." Mina had told Amber last night when they'd talked. "Anything about Yvonne?"

"I wish there was!"

"Maybe you should stay outside the study door while I slip inside with the iced tea? Who knows what evil I'll run into?"

"Oh, Amber. I know you think I'm getting what I deserve."

"Be right back, Lois Lane." Amber's jaw tightened as she carried the tray to the door.

Molly paced the kitchen, her heart hammering.

Amber walked to the study, took a deep breath and walked in. Quinn sat on the sofa beside Yvonne Stoddard. Yvonne wore pale blue slacks and blouse, wide white belt and white high-heeled sandals. Amber smiled slightly as she set the tray on the coffee table.

"Thank you, Jane," said Quinn.

Amber nodded.

Yvonne looked sharply at Amber, but didn't speak to her.

Amber imagined the questions whirling inside Yvonne's head and she hid a smile. Each time Yvonne saw her she'd tried to place her, but so far had failed. In high school Amber's hair was styled in a short red cap and she was short and skinny, covered with freckles and dressed conservatively. During college she suddenly blossomed into what others called a real beauty. She let her hair grow to the middle of her back, had it permed, had learned how to dress to look her best and had even grown two inches taller. She knew the pink and white uniform she wore looked good on her.

Yvonne turned to Quinn. "I would like to stay for dinner, Quinn. May I?"

Amber filled the glasses with tea as she waited for Quinn to answer. She saw a muscle jump in his jaw.

Quinn took the glass that Amber held out to him. "The girls and I share dinner every evening, Yvonne. I explained that."

She opened her brown eyes wide and stuck out her red bottom lip as she pushed back her bleached blond hair. "I just want to be with you, Quinn. I won't keep you from the girls."

Amber slowly walked out. She heard Yvonne say sharply, "Quinn, that woman looks very familiar to me."

Amber stiffened.

"Jane does?" asked Quinn. "Mother hired her."

"I know. I don't know where I've seen her, but I'm sure I have."

Trembling, Amber walked back to the kitchen and stepped inside, her face pale.

Molly whirled around as Amber walked in. She caught Amber's arm. "You look ready to faint. It was Yvonne, wasn't it?"

"Yes." Amber sank to a kitchen chair and Molly sat in the chair beside her.

"Well?"

"She looked at me as if she knew me! But I acted like I didn't know her and she finally shrugged as if she'd been wrong. But she asked Quinn about me." Amber wiped her brow with a trembling hand. "It's a good thing you didn't walk in there. If she saw us together she'd figure out who I am."

"Did Quinn ask about me?"

"No."

"I'm glad!"

"Yvonne's probably staying for dinner. She invited herself and he didn't turn her down." Amber jabbed her fingers through her bright hair. "Since Mrs. Mathis is gone for a few days again Yvonne is going to take advantage of that. Mrs. Mathis often refused to let Yvonne stay even when she asked. Quinn doesn't have the guts that his mother has."

"Maybe he likes Yvonne."

"Maybe, but I doubt it. He's just very polite."

Molly jumped up and paced the room. "I have to do something, Amber. I can't very well have dinner with them." She tore a piece of notepaper off the pad beside the telephone and scribbled a note to Quinn, then handed it to Amber. "Take that to him. I've said that I'm taking the girls to the park and then out for a hamburger since he has company, and that I'll see him when I return."

"Smart girl." Amber took the note and folded it. "I think I'll pass it to him when the shark isn't looking."

"I'll talk to you later. I'd better get the girls before they decide to find Uncle Quinn." Molly dashed to the family room, stopped outside the door, took a deep breath and stepped inside. The girls looked up from watching TV. "How would you girls like to go play in the park a while and then go for a hamburger and shake?"

"Yes! We want to!"

"I'll run up and get my purse and be right back."

A few minutes later Molly started back down the stairs when she heard voices just below. She stopped dead in her tracks. Her legs trembled and she crept back up and looked down through the railing to see Yvonne and Quinn talking to the girls. Yvonne was trying to act as if she was interested in the children, but Molly could tell the girls could see right through her. Finally Quinn and Yvonne walked away and Molly sped down to the girls.

"Ready, girls?"

"Ready!" They ran ahead of her toward the back door.

"Molly."

At the sound of Quinn's voice Molly stopped dead, her heart in her mouth. Slowly she turned then, when she found Quinn alone, she breathed easier. "Yes?"

"I want you back here for dinner."

"But you have company."

He sighed and stabbed his fingers through his mass of dark hair. "I am having dinner with you and the girls."

"What about Mrs. Stoddard?"

"She's not coming."

Molly bit back a relieved sigh. "We'll be back later then."

He nodded, turned slowly and walked down the hall, his shoulders bent and his steps dragging.

Sympathy for him rose inside her and she wanted to call after him and tell him everything would be all right, but she didn't say anything. She walked to her yellow Mustang with the girls running beside her.

Later at dinner Molly lifted a bite of roast beef to her mouth just as Quinn said, "Yvonne will be having dinner with us Tuesday."

Molly's fork clattered to her plate. She flushed and quickly picked it up. Finally Molly was able to say, "I've wanted to tell you that I'll be gone Tuesday evening. Something came up. I know Jane will take care of the girls for me." Did she sound as panicky as she felt?

Quinn frowned as he wadded his napkin. "I'm sorry to hear that. I told Yvonne what a special time we have each evening and she wanted to join us. I finally gave in and agreed to one dinner."

"And will that satisfy her?"

Quinn narrowed his eyes. "I think so."

"Do we have to have dinner with Mrs. Stoddard?" asked Deanie.

"I'd rather go to McDonald's with Molly," said Tonya.

Quinn shot Molly a knowing look, then smiled at the girls. "Please don't leave me alone, girls. I couldn't get along without you, especially since Molly will be gone. You can't ask me to entertain Mrs. Stoddard all on my own, can you?"

"You could tell her to stay home," said Tonya.

Quinn sighed. "I'll tell her to come just for dessert. I'm sure she'll understand."

"I'm sure." Molly hid a smile behind her napkin.

Just then the doorbell rang and Quinn frowned as he looked toward the hall. "Who can that be?"

"Yvonne Stoddard?" asked Molly in a low, tight voice that Quinn heard.

"I suppose it could be." Quinn sighed heavily. "She said she might come even after I asked her not to."

Abruptly Molly pushed back her chair. "Excuse me, please. I'm suddenly not feeling well at all." She ran to the kitchen before anyone could speak. She stopped just inside the kitchen door, her palms damp and her legs weak. Smells of roast beef and hot rolls hung in the air. She knew Amber had gone to answer the door.

Molly dropped to a chair and waited in silence until Amber ran back in. Her freckles stood out against her white face and she grabbed Molly's arm and shook it.

"You scared me out of my wits, Molly! I thought you were in the dining room. I tried to get Yvonne to go to the den to wait, but she wouldn't. She marched right into the dining room and I ran after her. When I saw your place empty I turned and ran back out. They must've thought I was very strange."

"I ran out when I heard the doorbell. I was afraid it'd be Yvonne."

"It was. The one and only." Amber sank to her

chair and leaned her elbows on the table. "She was dressed in a red dress and looked ready to eat Quinn alive."

"Better him than me," said Molly with a shaky smile.

"One of these days she's going to see your car and then the game will be up." Amber fingered a napkin. "You said she knows your car. Why don't you have that serious talk with Quinn tonight?"

Molly's stomach tightened and she shook her head. "I just can't yet."

"I saw her heading for the garage yesterday. I headed her off, but she's a real snoop and if it's your car she was looking for, she'll find it sooner or later. She said she wanted to make sure Quinn was home before she came to the door, but I didn't believe her."

Molly leaned back weakly. "She wouldn't know to look for my car here."

"Maybe not, but she is after something in that garage and I wish I knew what," said Amber. "and she's determined to meet you, the elusive Molly Lynn. She called to ask me about you, but I acted dumb."

"Maybe I could use Jack's pickup for a while."

"Molly, Molly." Amber shook her head. "How far will you go?"

"You're right, Amber. I must tell Quinn. And I will. I promise. I just don't know when. Or how. Oh, is a story really worth all of this?" She pushed away from the table and slowly walked outdoors to stand in the shade of a giant maple with the wind ruffling the leaves. A lone tear slipped down her cheek.

Amber sighed. Was Molly falling in love with Quinn Mathis? "I don't have time to think about that. I'd better get to Steve's study while everyone is busy." She had decided that if she couldn't find the key tonight she'd call a locksmith in the morning. Mrs. Mathis wanted to keep everything quiet, but she must realize it wasn't always possible.

Amber stopped just inside the study, closed the door, clicked on the light and slowly looked around. She had looked inside, under and on top of everything in the entire house for the missing key. She felt along the hem of the wide drapes that were drawn across the glass door. She had even looked in the garage. Mina had said she would come and find it for her, but Amber told her it would look too suspicious.

As usual her gaze fell on the picture that covered the wall safe. This time she looked at the objects on the antique table; a small wooden box, a brass candle holder, a key and a pair of old spectacles.

"The key!" she whispered. She ran to the picture and touched the key. It felt smooth. She pulled the footstool under the picture and stood on it, then peered closely at the key. She tried to pick it off the canvas. It looked real, but it wasn't. "Am I crazy, or what?" she muttered.

She ran her fingers around the frame. "Nothing." She pressed the frame just below the key. Something under her fingers moved. "What do you know," she whispered. She pressed the frame again and a tiny section of it dropped down to reveal a small key hanging on a tiny hook. She lifted the key off and pushed the section of the frame back in place.

A few minutes later she had unlocked the hidden door and opened it. Inside she saw three small boxes gift-wrapped in birthday paper. Tonya, Deanie and Barb's names were printed on the cards attached to them. Beside the gifts was a collection of old coins. On the bottom shelf she saw a gray notebook that didn't seem important enough to lock away in a hidden place. Her heart raced as she lifted out the gray notebook.

"What have we here?"

She opened it. In Steve's careful handwriting she read dates and times of meetings with Al Wilkens and amounts of money used. She frowned thoughtfully. "Al Wilkens?"

She flipped the page. "Ah! Wilkens' Appliance Store! That's where I heard the name before. So, gambling is the key here."

She turned another page and a paper fluttered to the floor. She picked it up and read, "$10,000 to be paid to Al Wilkens within ninety days." It was dated and signed by Mark Petersen.

Again she looked at the book. Steve had listed his losses as well as Mark Petersen's. On another page he listed the names of the people involved. Amber glanced over the list. Her eyes narrowed as she spotted Yvonne Stoddard's name.

"So, that's the connection. Yvonne must be looking for this book."

Amber slipped the paper back in place, closed the book and held it to her. She closed and locked the secret door, put the key in place and walked to her room off the kitchen. The puzzle was finally falling into place. But it didn't look good for Steve Mathis.

Chapter 7

He ran a finger down her cheek. "Your mind is wandering again, Molly."

"What?" She looked at Dale as he set the picnic basket on an empty park bench, dragged her attention back to him and smiled. "Sorry. I was thinking about work. What were you saying?"

"I missed you this past week. You called me twice and couldn't talk long either time; now your mind is off somewhere instead of here with me. I missed you." He slipped an arm around her and she stiffened.

"Did you really, Dale?"

"Of course."

She sighed. "I missed you, too."

"That's better, Molly," he whispered as he kissed her. "I love you."

She studied him closely, looking for something, but not knowing what. He looked the same with his blond hair combed neatly, his immaculate suit and shirt that he'd worn to church, his nice smile, his beautiful blue eyes, and his weak chin. She frowned slightly. "Do you really love me, Dale?" She saw the sudden hurt look on his face and she laughed lightly. "I don't know why I asked." She dropped her purse on the picnic table, then sat down carefully to keep from snagging her yellow cotton slacks on the rough bench.

"I'm sorry we couldn't find a better table," said Dale. He looked around the crowded park at the laughing, talking people. Children played Frisbee and soccer and a few men played football. "All the other tables were taken."

"I don't mind at all. It's a beautiful, sunny day for a picnic and we won't let an old bench ruin it for us." She kissed his cheek and he hugged her tightly for a moment, then released her to open the picnic basket.

A slight breeze ruffled his blond hair, making him look more approachable. He turned to Molly with the plates in his hand. "I still don't see why you won't give me your phone number."

Her mind raced for an answer he could accept without further questions. "I told you I'm on an undercover assignment."

"I hate not being able to call you!"

"I know, but it shouldn't be much longer." She lifted out a thermos and glasses. "Tell me about your week."

He frowned thoughtfully. "I don't know what's happening but something strange is going on at Ardetts.'

She gripped the glasses tightly, but forced her voice to stay light. "Oh? Strange how?"

He hesitated. "This cannot appear across the top of the *Freburg News* tomorrow."

"It won't."

"Quinn Mathis asked for a complete audit." Dale looked all around to make sure no one overheard him and he lowered his voice. "And money is missing. About fifty thousand."

She gasped. No wonder Quinn had been so disturbed. Was this what Amber Ainslie was working on? "Who could've taken it, Dale?"

"I don't know." He rubbed his hair back over his

ear. "It's causing quite a stir."

"Who had a motive?"

"I don't know."

"I'm surprised none of this leaked to the newspapers."

Dale gripped her arm. "Promise you won't say anything to your paper, Molly! Promise!"

"Dale!" She pried his fingers loose and rubbed the red spot on her wrist. "I already told you that I wouldn't say anything."

"I know. But sometimes you get carried away with this job of yours." He lifted out a packet of fried chicken and a bowl of cole slaw.

"Oh, Dale. You know I'm serious about my career, but I wouldn't print something that you told me in confidence." She thought of the things Quinn had told her and that she was indeed going to print, and she squirmed uneasily.

He hugged her again, then turned back to the food. "I'm hungry, aren't you? Mother made her own special fried chicken for us. And cole slaw with raisins and carrots."

Molly wrinkled her nose. Why couldn't Dale or his mother remember that she didn't like cole slaw made that way?

"Apple pie, too, Molly. Mother really outdid herself this time. I think she's beginning to like you."

Molly rolled her eyes, but didn't say anything.

A soccer ball rolled against her foot and she easily kicked it back to the boy chasing it. He shouted thanks and ran back to his game. Molly bit into a piece of fried chicken. "It's delicious."

"I'll be sure to tell Mother."

Molly ate without speaking as she watched children play and other people eat at nearby tables.

Dale wiped his fingers and said, "Did I tell you

about the new girl working for me?"

"No. I don't think so."

"She just moved here from Montana and she has no friends. Her name is Nora Bates and she's small and delicate and the best little worker I've ever had. She seems to read my mind. I ... I showed her around town last night."

"That's nice."

"You don't mind?"

"Why should I? Hey, maybe she's our answer."

"To what?"

"When we have our honeymoon she can take over your department until we get back and you won't be so nervous about being gone."

The color drained from his face and he stiffened. "We aren't even engaged, Molly. How can you talk about a honeymoon?"

"Dale, I'm so tired of waiting. I want to get married. Don't you want the same?"

He tugged his tie loose. "Of course I do, Molly. But not now."

She leaned close to him and whispered hoarsely, "Dale, do you really love me?"

"Of course I do," he said stiffly. A muscle jumped in his jaw.

"Then let's get married now, not next year, but now! Please!"

"Stop it, Molly. You'll ruin our day."

Tears sparkled in her eyes.

He pulled her close and rested his cheek against hers. "We'll probably get married, Molly. But not now."

"I'm ... I'm scared, Dale. I'm scared if we don't get married now, we never will." She lifted her face and a tear slipped down her cheek.

"Oh, Molly! Don't look at me like that." He

touched his lips to her trembling ones and she wrapped her arms around him.

Just then a movement behind Dale caught her attention and she looked over his shoulder. The color drained from her face. Quinn Mathis stood under a tree watching her, watching them kiss. Quinn bent his head to acknowledge her, then turned away to get the girls playing nearby.

Flushing with guilt, Molly pushed away from Dale. "I want to leave, Dale."

"But why? We have so much to talk about."

She stood up, tucking her blouse neatly into her slacks. "I have to go back to work and I need to rest first."

Dale caught her hand. "Just give me your phone number so I can call you during the week."

She shook her head. "I can't. I'll call you. I promise I will." She dropped the thermos into the open basket. "Drive me home now, Dale."

He jammed things into the basket, his face dark with anger. "I hope you realize that you ruined my day."

"I know and I'm sorry."

"You should be."

"Please, Dale, don't be difficult."

He sighed heavily. "I'm sorry. Are you sure about tomorrow night?"

She nodded. "I already told you I can't go to Ardetts' picnic with you. But I'll be there."

"All right, but I just might make other plans."

"Such as?"

He shrugged. "I'll take you home now. I told Nora I might drop in on her today."

"Fine."

"You don't mind?"

"Of course not!"

About eight that night Molly parked her car in the Mathis's six-car garage and sat quietly for a minute. After a long afternoon and evening alone she'd reached a decision. Somehow she'd have to find the courage to face Quinn and tell him the truth about herself. She couldn't deceive him any longer or she wouldn't be able to live with herself.

Slowly she walked inside and found Quinn and the girls watching TV in the family room.

"Hi," she said, butterflies fluttering in her stomach as she pushed her glasses in place. Had Quinn noticed that she wasn't wearing glasses at the park with Dale?

"Hi," said the girls, smiling in delight at seeing her, but immediately going back to watching TV.

Quinn stood at the brick fireplace, his face thoughtful, his dark eyes alert. His light blue tee shirt stretched across his broad shoulders and pressed smoothly against his flat, hard stomach. His faded jeans fit snugly against his long legs to end at the top of his sock-covered feet. He nodded at her without speaking, but his eyes spoke volumes. Weakly she sank to the couch before her legs gave way.

Quinn stepped toward her with the lithe grace of a panther. "So, you look different when you're not with us."

She shrugged and pushed back a stray strand of hair that had escaped her bun.

"Was that the man you're going to marry?

She barely nodded, her heart thudding so loud she was sure he could hear it. Absently she picked at a thread on the seam of her jeans. She should tell Quinn right out that he knew the man, in fact, he worked for Quinn, but the words refused to come.

"When's the wedding date?" He walked with easy grace to the couch and sat with his knee bent, facing her. His nearness made her tremble with a feeling she couldn't, or wouldn't, define.

"Nothing definite," she said just above a whisper.

"You promised me six months."

She moistened her dry lips with the tip of her tongue, ready to ask him for a private meeting in the study.

He narrowed his eyes. "Being with us is more than just a job to you, isn't it, Molly?"

She lifted her brow questioningly, still unable to speak properly.

Quinn leaned forward slightly. She could smell the scent of his skin and every nerve-end tingled with awareness. "It's a relationship with this family, Molly. You're important to us, to the girls."

She looked away and stared at her guitar standing beside his in the corner. A strange feeling that she couldn't understand tugged at her heart. She turned her head and his eyes locked with hers, almost unwillingly, as if compelled by a force he couldn't control. Time seemed to stand still and her breast rose and fell in agitation. Finally he looked away and she could breathe again.

Quinn cleared his throat. "I've been meaning to ask you about the Boys' Club, Molly."

"Oh?"

"I need you to help me with them, if you would." His voice was a shade gruff. When he turned back toward her, his eyes were impersonal once again and his manner brisk. "Before you agree, keep in mind that it'll take up a great deal of your time."

"What do you want me to do?" It was hard to keep her voice level, to respond as if nothing had passed between them. Maybe nothing had. Maybe it was her over-active imagination.

Quinn stabbed his fingers through his dark hair.

"Our church started a club for boys and it's grown to about five hundred boys now. Several men in the area work with the boys and I told them that I would take the boys that Steve had arranged to take. Ten ten-year-olds are coming here for a campout. I can't possibly handle it without your help. What do you say?"

She moved restlessly. Here was one more tangle of the web she was weaving. "I must talk to you privately first, Quinn. You might not want my help after you hear what I have to say."

"Nonsense!" The clock on the mantle bonged and Quinn jumped up. "I'm sorry, but I have an appointment. I didn't realize it was so late. We'll talk later, Molly." He kissed the girls goodnight, lifted his hand to Molly, and strode out, taking the very life in the room with him.

Molly slumped against the couch with a ragged sigh. She didn't know if she was more glad he'd left or simply aggravated to have her plans to tell the truth thwarted once again.

The girls laughed at the comedy on TV, but Molly couldn't find anything funny. Finally she pushed herself up. "Girls, I'm going to find Jane and talk to her. I'll be back later."

The girls nodded, but didn't look up.

Molly walked listlessly to Amber's room and knocked lightly on the closed door. Amber opened the door with a flourish, then wrinkled her nose and shook her head.

"You're not Mina," she said, stepping aside. "She said she has something to tell me."

Molly looped her thumbs in her jeans pockets. "I could come another time if you don't have time for an old friend who's in a great deal of trouble."

Amber laughed and closed the door. "What's up

that has you so down?"

"Don't ask!"

"Don't ask, she says!" Amber motioned for Molly to sit on the rocker while she took the small couch. "All I ask is that when Mina does come, you quickly excuse yourself and leave without a trace of dust."

Molly laughed and felt better. "I can do that. I should feel bad that you don't trust me enough to let me know what Mina has to report."

Amber waved her hand. "Now, tell me what's bothering you so much. As if I didn't know."

Molly locked her hands around her knees and leaned forward. "Amber, I need to know everything you know about the accident."

"Why now? What happened?"

"I don't think I'll be here much longer, Amber. You know that I'm going to tell Quinn the truth, and I mean to do it soon. I tried just now, but he had to leave." Molly fingered the gold chain at her neck. "Once he knows the truth, I'm out of here on my ear, so please, tell me what you know!"

Amber traced a flower on her skirt and the smile left her face. "Why can't you forget about the Mathis story, and just stay here with the girls? Put your writing aside for a while."

"I can't! Amber, I just can't! Please, tell me what you know."

Amber reached for a throw pillow and hugged it to her. After a long silence she said, "I promised Barney that I wouldn't tell anyone what I'm going to tell you."

"I'm sorry. But I must know."

"Barney told me that when Steve Mathis left here with his wife, the brakes of the car were in perfect working order. That's part of Barney's job, to see that the cars are in top shape. Barney said that he'd taken the car to Jack's garage just the day before. You remember Jack from school." Molly nodded and Amber continued. "Jack said that everything was perfect. Barney drove the car home without any problem with the brakes. Steve and Barb drove to a party for the office staff of Ardetts. Obviously, they arrived there with no problem. When they drove home *after* the party, the brakes failed. The car crashed and they were both killed." Amber's voice faded away.

"Do the police know this?"

"Yes."

"Do they know who tampered with the brakes?"

Amber shook her head. "No. They aren't convinced that anyone tampered with the brakes. But I'm sure someone did, and whoever did it must be found."

Molly rocked gently for a minute. "Tomorrow evening is the Ardetts' picnic. That would give me a good chance to talk to the people who work at Ardetts."

"Are you forgetting that many of those people know who you are?"

"You're right. I'll just make sure I tell Quinn the truth before then."

"And he'll keep you away from the picnic, and maybe out of this town."

Molly lifted her chin and her eyes snapped. "The park is public property. He can't keep me from being there. Besides, I'll be singing."

"Oh, Molly, please forget this. Let me handle it."

"I want the story, Amber! I need it."

"Why?"

"For a lot of reasons. I don't know. I just need it." Molly jumped up and paced the floor, then stopped in front of Amber. "What else do you know? You told me what Mina said, but I know there's something that you know."

Amber shook her head.

"Amber! Please, please, tell me!"

"It was Steve Mathis."

"Yes?"

"Mina said someone saw him arguing with a man about ... about gambling debts!"

"Steve Mathis? I don't believe it!"

"They were arguing and the man grabbed Steve by the front of his shirt and said if he didn't pay what he owed him, that he'd kill Steve."

"What did the man look like?"

"I don't know. It was dark and my source couldn't see him well enough to identify him. But Steve walked into the light and that's how he was recognized."

Molly pursed her lips and stood at the window looking out across the yard. Finally she turned. "Thanks, Amber. I promise to keep this to myself until I learn just what it means in the mystery."

"Thanks. I know I shouldn't have said anything." Amber laced her fingers together. What would Molly say if she knew the whole truth?

Just then Mina knocked at the door.

"I'll get out of here," said Molly.

Amber opened the door and Mina sailed in. Wind had tangled her bright curls and reddened her round cheeks.

Mina shook her finger at Molly. They had met Thursday evening. "You might like to know that I caught Yvonne Stoddard heading toward the garage just now. I stopped her before she looked inside."

Molly clamped her hand to her mouth and her blue eyes widened. "Do you think she was looking for my car?"

"I doubt it, Molly." Amber pushed back her red hair with a freckled hand. "She has no idea who you are. If she had seen it, we'd all have heard about it by now."

"I wonder what she wants in the garage?" asked Mina.

"I wish I knew," said Molly. "She's certainly not the mechanical type."

"But she's snoopy," said Amber. "She probably wanted to see the year of Quinn's Cadillac so she could buy a newer one."

"But she already drives a Mercedes," said Molly.

"Some people want everything," said Mina.

Molly nodded. "See you later." She walked out, closing the door behind her.

Amber waited for a minute, then showed Mina the notebook she had found. "Mina, I want you to find all you can on Al Wilkens, Mark Petersen and Yvonne Stoddard. If you need help, ask Carol at my office."

In the kitchen Molly poured herself a glass of lemonade and sipped it slowly. At a step behind her she spun around. "Oh, Quinn, you surprised me. Can I get you a lemonade?"

"I can manage, thanks."

She watched his strong, lean hands as he poured out two glasses of lemonade and set them on a tray. She bit her bottom lip and gathered all of her courage. "Quinn, is it possible for us to have a talk later?"

"Maybe, but Yvonne is here now."

Molly lifted a fine brow.

"I don't know how long it'll take me to get rid of her." He grinned and shook his head. "Strike that from the record, please."

"Done," she said with a laugh.

He walked to the door with the tray in his hands, then turned. "Molly, before I forget again, would you please plan to take the girls to the Ardetts' picnic tomorrow? I can't watch them since I'll be occupied with other things and Mother won't be back in time."

"What about . . . about Mrs. Stoddard?"

"She'll be out of town, she said, so I really am counting on you."

Molly nodded. "I'll do it."

Later, after she told him the truth, he wouldn't want her with the girls. But she was already committed to sing for the entertainment at the picnic, and that would give her a good excuse for being there. She nodded again. "Yes, I'll be there."

"Good. I knew you wouldn't let me down."

"I do need to speak with you privately, soon."

He sighed heavily. "Right now I have so much on my mind that I doubt if I'd be a very good listener even if I had the time. But we'll talk. One of these days I might even have more time to spend with the girls."

"They'll like that."

"So will I. They're special. I think you know that."

She smiled and nodded.

He eyed her closely. "I hope our private talk doesn't concern your wanting out of our agreement before the six months are up, Molly."

"No. Not at all."

"Good." He looked relieved. "Can you give me a hint?"

"It's something I have to sit down and discuss with you. It takes time."

He shrugged. "I'll have to be content with that. Talk to you later."

"Later." As he left she leaned weakly against the counter and forced her heartbeat to slow down. She should have blurted out the truth and taken the consequences. She shook her head. "No, I must tell him carefully and slowly."

Chapter 8

Monday at the picnic she wished that she had told Quinn the truth as people she knew greeted her. Thankfully none of them spoke her last name, and she felt somewhat safe. None of them asked about her job as a reporter, but several of them asked about Dale. "I'm looking for him," she answered each time. He had been angry with her when he learned that she wouldn't attend the picnic with him.

With the girls beside her, Molly watched children run and shout in the park. Teens, along with some of the adults, played tennis and softball. Women placed dishes of food on several tables which were pushed together under the shade of giant oaks. The sun burned hot against Molly's skin and she was thankful that she wore shorts and a suntop much like Deanie and Tonya. Laughter and music from a tape player filled the air making the park ring with sounds.

Molly looked down at the girls and said, "I see three little girls at the swings that you can meet. It'll be fun to play with them."

"Let's run!" Deanie pulled on Molly's hand, and together the three of them ran to the swings.

Tonya looked around, then tugged on Molly's arm as Molly retied the tie on Deanie's sunsuit strap. "Look, Molly. There's Uncle Quinn. *She's* with him."

Molly looked and her heart plunged to her feet to find Yvonne talking with Quinn near the grills. Yvonne wore a white jumpsuit that looked out of place in the park, and high-heeled sandals.

"Let's go talk to him," said Deanie.

"He's busy right now," said Molly, forcing her voice to sound normal. "We'll swing a while first. I want you to meet these three girls." Quickly she introduced Deanie and Tonya to the girls on the swings. They talked and laughed, leaving Molly free to walk to the bench facing the swings and away from the grills.

"What am I going to do?" she whispered, shivering in the heat. Somehow she had to stay away from Quinn and Yvonne.

She saw Dale's car turn into the park and she jumped up, ready to run to Dale for help. As he drove past she tried to get his attention with a wave. She saw that he was engrossed with a woman in the passenger seat beside him and didn't notice her. She frowned.

He parked next to a red compact and Molly watched as he walked around and opened the door for his passenger. A petite woman with short brown hair, dressed in jeans and a western shirt, slipped out and stood beside him, looking up at him with a look of adoration that Molly could see even at that distance. Dale slipped an arm around her small waist and ushered her to the back of the car where he opened the trunk and took out a basket of food. Together they carried it to the tables. Molly clenched her fists and took great breaths of air. She stood uncertainly as Dale walked the woman across the park toward her. He was too deep in conversation to see her standing directly in front of him. Finally he lifted his head, saw her and flushed beet-red.

"Oh, Molly. Hello," he said. "I want you to meet Nora Bates. I told you that she just moved here from Montana."

"Hello, Nora."

"Hi, Molly. I'm so glad to meet a friend of Dale's." Nora held out her hand and smiled brightly. "You don't work at Ardetts, do you?"

"No."

Nora smiled and squeezed Dale's arm. "I'm thankful that I can work with Dale."

"You're a good worker," said Dale softly.

Molly saw the look on his face and jealousy rose inside her. She abruptly excused herself and walked away.

"It was very nice to meet you," Nora called after her.

Dale led her away while Molly stood at the bench, her head bent. A hand touched her shoulder and she jumped. She looked up into Quinn's face and trembled.

"What's wrong, Molly?"

"Dale Gerard brought someone else today! How could he do that to me after all this time? Will a little girl from Montana break us up?"

"Is Dale Gerard the man you're going to marry?" Quinn's voice shook with emotion.

Molly's anger died, and her face turned almost as white as the fluffy clouds in the summer blue sky. She dropped to the bench, trembling, and stared speechlessly up at Quinn.

He sank down beside her, his arm across the back of the bench, his jean-clad knee bent so he could face her. His brows almost reached his hairline and his dark eyes pinned her to the spot. "Dale Gerard, Molly?"

"Yes," she whispered.

"I had no idea. He works for me."

"I know."

"Why didn't you mention it?"

"Would it have made a difference?" It was hard to breathe with him so close to her. She saw a muscle jump in his jaw.

"I don't know. He doesn't seem your type. I can't imagine you being in love with him."

"Oh?"

Quinn leaned toward her and his breath fanned her face. "You'd overpower him. He needs someone like little Nora Bates."

"What do you know about it? I love Dale and he loves me!"

"I happen to know he's not engaged, nor does he have plans to be engaged. I talked to him just the other day. It seems the man is not in love. And if you looked closely in your heart, you'd see that you're not in love with him."

Her temper flared and she narrowed her flashing eyes. "We're saving money for the marriage," she said icily. "You wouldn't understand since you never have money problems."

He squeezed her shoulder, and his touch burned into her flesh. "Molly, I'm surprised at your choice of men." His eyes darkened. "I am sorry that you're hurt. You'll get over it."

Her face crumpled and she burst into tears. He pressed a handkerchief into her hands and she took it, wiped her eyes and forced back the flow. "I . . . I don't want to get over it. I've waited so long now! It's not fair." She lifted wide blue eyes to his. "If you loved a woman you wouldn't wait years before you married her, would you? You'd sweep her off her feet and marry her fast. Wouldn't you?"

He rubbed a hand across his face. "What makes

you think so?"

"I think I know you pretty well, Quinn. I know that you'd go after what you want."

"Would I now?"

Should she tell him the truth right now? "Quinn?"

"Yes."

"I'm . . ." She lost her voice. Before she could force it back, Yvonne called to Quinn from the sidewalk. Molly froze, unable to turn her head and have Yvonne recognize her.

Quinn pushed himself up and stood stiffly. "Yes, Yvonne."

Molly waited for the ground to open up and swallow her but, to her disappointment, it didn't happen.

Yvonne walked across the grass and stopped just a foot away. "Molly? Is that really you, Molly?"

Slowly Molly stood, squared her shoulders and stood beside Quinn to face Yvonne. "Hello, Yvonne."

Yvonne looked from Quinn to Molly. "I didn't know you two knew each other. Just what are you up to this time, Molly DuPree?"

Quinn frowned down at Molly. "DuPree?"

Molly looked helplessly at him, dreading the look in his eyes.

Yvonne laughed a tinkling, silvery laugh. "Don't you know you're talking to the ace reporter of the *Freburg News*? She always gets her story. The Lois Lane of Freburg." Yvonne lifted a fine brow. "Didn't you know, Quinn?"

Molly held her breath, searching for the right words to say at such an awkward moment. None came to mind.

Quinn's eyelids hooded his dark eyes to block out their message. "I know Molly very well," he said coldly.

"You'd better watch every word you say around her or you'll find it splashed all over the front of the paper." Yvonne slipped her hand in Quinn's arm. "Let's get back to the grill. People are waiting for hamburgers."

He looked at Molly, his face set. "We'll talk later."

She barely nodded, her voice gone, and her legs trembling.

"Goodbye, Molly," said Yvonne. "I saw Dale with another woman. Having trouble holding your man? I thought you would."

With one last knowing look Quinn turned from Molly and walked across the grass with Yvonne clinging to him and chattering gaily. Molly sank to the bench. She shoved her glasses into her purse and locked her hands in her lap as shivers ran up and down her back. The worst had happened. Quinn knew the truth about her. Now she would be sent flying out of his home and out of his life.

The girls dropped onto the grass at Molly's feet, breathing heavily from running. "We're thirsty, Molly," said Deanie.

Molly pulled herself together enough to take the girls to the water frountain and watch them drink long, gulping drinks. She glanced at her watch and groaned. It was almost time for her to sing. "Let's go to the band shelter so I can tune my guitar, girls."

They each grabbed one of her hands and pulled her across the grass. A bird flew from the ground to a tree branch. A car on the street honked loud and long.

"Sit here, girls," she said, placing them in the second row of seats. "As soon as I can, I'll join you." She pulled out the skirt she'd packed, dropped her bag on a chair next to Tonya, then walked to the platform where her guitar waited. With trembling hands she tied her yellow wrap-around skirt around her narrow waist, then lifted her acoustic guitar out of the case and tuned it, listening closely to each pluck of the strings. Several people called and waved to her and she waved back. A big man with western boots and shirt, faded jeans, and a big mustache walked up to join her.

"Hi, Rex." She smiled.

"All set, Molly? You look a little peaked. You all right?"

"Sure."

"I hope you know you're the favorite on our list of performers this year. Several people requested you after last year's grand performance." He picked up a banjo and walked to a tall wooden stool. He plucked the banjo, then tuned it with her guitar. "Let's do some pickin' before the crowd gathers for the show, Molly girl."

She adjusted her strap, lifted herself to the stool, and nodded. Somehow she'd have to forget the incident with Quinn and concentrate on the music. She strummed the guitar and Rex joined in with banjo picking that set her toes tapping. Soon she was lost in the music. Her eyes sparkled and her cheeks grew rosy. A crowd gathered and she barely noticed. Bluegrass, gospel and classical were all favorites of hers and she and Rex played them well.

When they finally stopped, the applause was loud and long. Her head shot up, then she grinned. Rex chuckled and walked to the microphone.

"That was extra for all you early birds," he said with a laugh that boomed out loud and clear. "It was just pure fun, but now we'll start this musical affair that you came to hear and enjoy." He beamed at the audience and they shouted and clapped. Then he flashed a toothy grin at Molly. "Since our Molly's already up here, we'll put her right to work. Folks, give this pretty lady a warm welcome today while she comes to sing some of our favorites."

Molly ran the few steps to the mike, bowed slightly, adjusted one mike for her height and another for her guitar while the audience clapped and stomped and whistled. She smiled and the group grew quiet. As she started playing she looked at the people sitting on the chairs and standing around the edge of the pavilion. Her eyes locked with Quinn's and for a second the smile faltered, but she forced her gaze away. Deanie held up her hand beside her glowing face and waved a tiny wave. Molly winked at her. She would sing as if Quinn wasn't listening and watching, as if her world hadn't collapsed.

She could feel love flowing from her as she sang song after song. The words and the haunting melodies reached out and touched hearts and the applause was louder and longer than before. After the last song, she bowed low, then carried her guitar back to sit on a chair beside Rex. Her hands trembled as she leaned her guitar against her legs, holding the neck securely.

Rex ran to the mike. "This next musician is a surprise to all of you today. He asked me to keep it his secret and I managed to do just that. Please welcome our big boss himself, Quinn Mathis."

Molly gasped as the crowd roared. Her stomach fluttered as she watched him walk to the dark-stained guitar and pick it up. Instead of walking to the mike, he walked to her.

"Molly, come play and sing with me," he said with a smile that didn't reach his eyes.

"I . . . I couldn't."

"You will!" he whispered harshly. "Now!"

Unsteadily she walked to the mike with him.

"You sing melody and I'll take the harmony just the way we do at home," he said so that it went out over the mike.

She flushed red to the roots of her hair as she hooked her guitar strap and stood beside him waiting for his cue.

He started picking a gospel song that they'd sung just a few nights ago. With a deliberate movement he turned to face her so that she'd have to look at him while they sang. A hush fell over the crowd and together Molly and Quinn sang, their voices blending in perfect harmony. The audience went wild and Quinn immediately started another song. When it was finished he bowed to the audience, then to Molly. She smiled and curtsied prettily. Together they bowed again to the audience. Quinn slipped a strong arm around her narrow waist and she turned her head to stare at him in surprise. He bent his head and touched his lips to hers in a kiss that held her rooted to the spot.

"Thataway, boss," shouted several people from the crowd.

Molly's heart thudded loudly and she would have fallen if Quinn hadn't kept his arm around her as he bowed once again. Finally he released her and she walked to her chair and sank down. Quinn sat beside her, his arm over the back of her chair.

"Molly DuPree," he said against her ear. "I will see you at home."

Chapter 9

After a long, warm shower Molly dressed carefully in a bold print dress that clung to her curves and swirled around her legs. With a steady hand she applied eye makeup that turned her blue eyes into unforgettable sapphires. She brushed on blush and smoothed on lip color. When she finished with her hair it waved and curled wildly around her head and down her back. The butterfly had completely emerged and Quinn would notice and realize that she would not tremble and cower under his onslaught.

A chill ran down her spine. She ignored it as she squared her shoulders, lifted her chin and walked out of the bedroom and down the wide stairs, leaving a trail of perfume.

The house was quiet with the girls already asleep for the night. Only she and Quinn were up and awake and ready for battle. She stopped outside the closed study door and listened. Every nerve-end tingled. He was inside. She knew it without knowing how she knew it.

She raised her hand to knock, decided not to, then turned the knob, pushed open the door and sailed inside. The fire of battle was in her eyes, her movements, her very being.

Quinn whipped around from staring out the wide

glass door, his face dark with anger. He wore a three-piece blue pinstripe suit with a blue and red tie. He was dressed for battle, too.

Tension grew as they sized each other up. She took a step toward him as he took two toward her. They both stopped. Sparks flew from her eyes to clash against the anger in his.

"Molly DuPree!" He spit out the name. "So, is this the real you?"

She lifted her chin a fraction more. "Yes!"

"And I took you to be a Christian!"

"I am!"

"A liar!"

"I'm sorry for that."

"You used me! You used the girls! For what? A story! Why haven't I seen your by-line in the paper? Are you waiting to tell all? To have an entire spread?"

She doubled her fists at her sides. "I asked you for an interview time after time. You wouldn't allow me inside your office at Ardetts or here at your home. There's a story behind your brother's death and I intend to get it."

He stepped half a step forward. "How much sneaking around did you have to do here? Did you peek through my keyhole or listen at closed doors? Have you managed to look through my desk and my file cabinet?" He stabbed his fingers through his dark hair, then flipped back his jacket and stood with his hands on his hips, his feet apart. "Is there any part of my privacy you didn't invade?"

"I tried to tell you who I was and why I was here, but you didn't have time to listen." Her voice rose and she knew in a minute she'd be shouting at him. She took a deep breath, and brought her voice back down an octave. "I did not snoop around. I only want to learn the truth and report it."

"Distort it!"

She narrowed her eyes. "I happen to be a very good reporter. I do not distort the news!"

"Oh, I remember every seemingly innocent question you asked me about Steve and about Ardetts and the brakes on the car! I remember the cozy little chat we had when I let it slip that I was going to audit Ardetts! I remember almost every word you've ever said to me!" He stepped closer and she fell back a step. "Why didn't you tell me the truth then? We had time then!"

She shook her head. What could she say?

He tugged at his tie. "You fooled me all right. You made a fool of me. How do you think I felt when Yvonne sprang that on me today? Do you think I wanted her to guess what you'd done to me?"

"I am sorry. I know it must hurt your pride."

"My pride! Do you think that's all there is to it?" He growled deep in his throat and a shiver of fear passed through her. "What do you know of a man? You can't convince poor Dale Gerard to marry you and you have to use tricks to find stories for your newspaper. Something is wrong with you. You're a failure as a woman and as a reporter!"

"That's a cheap shot!" She stepped right up to him, her head back so that she could look him in the eye. "I could help solve the mystery that surrounds your brother's death. I could keep you from getting emotionally involved with that witch Yvonne Stoddard! I could do a lot of things for you if you'd only tell me what you know!"

"Why bring Yvonne into this?"

"You brought her up! She brought herself up when she exposed me today. I wanted to tell you about myself, but she beat me to it. Don't think she didn't guess that something was going on under that calm exterior of yours. She's been practicing deceit for years and she has it down to a fine art now. But you wouldn't know that, would you? All you see is the beautiful package that her expensive clothes wrap her in."

"Jealous, Molly?" His voice was deadly calm.

Her eyes widened. "Jealous? Of her? I most certainly am not!"

"We're getting off the subject here. We're talking about you and your deceit. We're talking about how you slithered your way into this house and my trust." He slammed his fist into his palm and she jumped. "How could you fool me like that? How could you get the girls to love you and trust you, knowing that you were going to leave them the minute you got the story?"

"You won't believe me, but I am sorry about that. I love the girls and I don't want to hurt them."

He leaned toward her and his breath was hot against her face. "Don't tell me you love them! You don't know the meaning of the word."

"I do love them," she said in a low voice. Tears pricked her eyes and she blinked them away. "I don't want to hurt them. I don't want to hurt you, either, Quinn."

"Next you'll be saying that you love me too." His mouth turned down and a muscle jumped in his jaw.

"I do care about you," she whispered.

His hands shot out and he gripped her arms. "How can you say that?"

His fingers bit into her delicate flesh and his hands burned into her arms. Without flinching she said, "I have learned what a fine man you are. I respect you and care about you."

"You lie! You don't care about me, only yourself! I want you out of my house, out of my life!"

She struggled, but she couldn't break free. "You're hurting me."

"You hurt me!"

"Let me go!"

Finally he dropped his hands. She flipped back her hair, challenging him further with the stance of her body and look in her eyes.

"Get out!" he roared. "Pack your bags and leave my house this instant."

She whirled around and ran to the door, then spun back to face him. "It's still not too late to ask me to stay for an interview. I could help you solve the mystery. If you'd ask."

"Out!" He flung out his arms, pointing toward the door. "Out!"

Butterflies fluttered in her stomach and her legs trembled until she thought she would fall, but she didn't let him see. "I could help you, Quinn. It doesn't have to end like this."

He doubled his fists at his sides and stepped toward her, his face dark with rage. She whirled around and ran down the hall and lightly up the stairs.

In her room she closed the door and leaned weakly against it, her head down and her heart hammering loud enough to drown out the ticking of the antique clock on the nightstand. Tears filled her eyes and slowly slipped down her ashen cheeks. Weakly she brushed them away but they continued to fall. She sniffed and rubbed the back of her hand across her nose. "I do care, Quinn," she whispered brokenly.

Finally she pulled her bags out of the closet and started to pack. Her legs felt like heavy weights and tears blurred her vision as she pushed under-wear and shirts and jeans into the bags. In one care-

less swoop she brushed her makeup into the case
with her toothbrush and travel mirror. She stopped
once to blow her nose and wipe away the tears. She
would wait to cry the rest of her tears in her own
place. She splashed cold water on her face and
patted it dry. With a ragged sigh she stacked her
bags together at the foot of her bed, then looked
around to make sure she hadn't left anything.
Once she was out of here, she'd never again be
allowed to set foot on Mathis property.

Dare she write a note to the girls and try to explain? Maybe she could leave a note for Amber,
asking her to talk to the girls.

Maybe Amber could still help her get the story
after Molly was gone.

Suddenly the door burst open and crashed against
the doorstop. Quinn strode in and stopped just
inches from her, a determined look on his face. Her
heart somersaulted, but she forced herself to stand
in place and not fall back in fright or weakness.

"Unpack your bags," he snapped. "You're staying."

She gasped. What could he mean?

"Don't just stand there with your mouth open.
Unpack your bags. You promised to stay here six
months and I am holding you to your word."

She sank to the edge of the bed, her eyes wide in
unbelief.

He reached out and pulled her to her feet. She
was too much in shock to object. "This could get
very noisy, I think. I don't want to wake the girls,
so we're going back to the study and get this settled
once and for all."

By the time they reached the door, her mind
cleared and she stopped. "I can walk on my own,
thank you."

His grip on her arm tightened. "We're going to

the study and I don't want to hear a word from you until we're inside with the door closed."

She sputtered but walked along beside him. Once inside he dropped her arm and she stumbled against the couch. In a flash she righted herself, her eyes blazing.

"I wouldn't stay here now if you asked, or begged me, Quinn Mathis! I'm going to get my things and drive away from here as fast as I can go."

He locked the study door and stood against it, his arms crossed, his face set. "No, you are not."

She clenched and unclenched her fists and her breast rose and fell. "Am I a prisoner?"

"If that's what you want to think. You're staying, Molly Lynn. Molly DuPree. You gave your word and I won't let you break it."

"You can't keep me here."

"Can't I?" She glanced at the glass door, then ran to it. Before she could unlock it his hands clamped around her slender waist. He lifted her easily and deposited her on the couch. She glared up at him, speechless and trembling. He really meant to keep her against her will!

He towered over her, his breathing ragged. "Are you ready to sit still and listen to me?"

She jumped up just inches from him. "Why are you doing this? Just let me go before I have to do something we'll both regret."

"You've already done something we both regret." Quinn clamped his hands to her shoulders and forced her back onto the couch. He sat beside her, one arm draped lightly over her shoulders, one hand holding her hands prisoners in her lap. She could smell the manly aroma of him and it made her head spin.

"Listen to me, Molly." His dark eyes bored into hers. "Listen!"

"No!" She shook her head. He waited. Finally she sagged back with a long, ragged sigh.

"That's better." But he didn't release her. Her heart raced with a new feeling that she couldn't define.

"Let me go," she said stiffly.

"Not yet."

Molly turned to face him. Her eyes locked with his and she couldn't breathe or move. She saw something flicker in his eyes, then disappear. Abruptly he released her and moved to the chair across from her. She rubbed her hands where his had gripped hers. Quinn propped his feet on the coffee table with his ankles crossed, his arms resting lightly on the arms of the chair. She knew that he wanted to appear relaxed, but she realized by the look in his eyes that he was still tense.

The clock chimed two and she jumped. From somewhere outdoors a dog barked. A sliver of moon hung in the sky just outside the window. Molly smoothed her skirt over her knees with trembling hands. Could Quinn hear the wild beat of her heart? What had made him suddenly change his mind about her staying?

"You are staying, Molly, because the girls need you." It was as if he could read her mind. She panicked at the thought.

"What about my job on the paper?"

"He shrugged. "It can wait."

She gasped. "It can't wait! It's my career!"

"That's too bad. What's five more months to you? The girls can't take another jolt just now. We both know it. They love you and trust you. Deanie still has nightmares occasionally. Tonya isn't herself yet. You're good for them. They're more important than your career." His voice was even and calm but he gripped the arms of the chair until his knuckles turned white. Seeing the look she gave him, he folded his arms across his broad chest. "The next few months are very important to their emotional well-being. I think you know that."

She nodded stiffly. "But I do think that we could bring someone else here and ease me out. Six months of my time is not necessary if we handle it correctly."

He dropped his feet to the floor and leaned forward. "Six months, Molly! You promised and I will not allow you to break that promise!"

She twisted a finger in her hair and bit her bottom lip. What could she say to make him relent?

"You'll stay here and continue to take care of the girls. If George Bailer won't give you a leave of absence, then you'll quit your job and put aside your career until your time here is over."

"You make it sound so simple." Her voice was bitter. "Don't I have any say in the matter?"

He shook his head, then leaned back again. "Make the most of it, Molly."

"What about my investigation?"

"Drop it."

"But I want to find out what happened to your brother. I want to know who took the money from Ardetts."

He pointed a long, lean finger at her. "You stay out of it! I mean it, Molly. I can handle it on my own."

"What about—the police?" She had almost asked about Amber, but knew Amber would be out too if he knew that he had a private detective working undercover right in his own house.

"I'm not going to sit back and wait for the police to make a move."

She slid to the edge of the couch and leaned forward earnestly. "I can help, Quinn." She saw the doubt on his face. "I can! I've been a reporter for almost five years and I know how to get information. You need me."

"No. No! It's dangerous." He shook his head. "I want you to take care of the girls and leave the mystery solving to me. I mean it. Molly? Do you hear me?"

She leaped up, her eyes flashing fire. "You are so stubborn! Don't you understand that I can help? I want to help!"

"You aren't going to."

"I don't have to listen to you. I can do what I want. I'm a free agent."

He shrugged and pushed himself up with easy grace. "The subject is closed, Molly DuPree. You're going to bed so that you can be up with the girls in the morning."

"No, Quinn. I'm going home. Right now."

He chuckled and the sound of it sent chills down her spine. Before she knew what he planned, he lifted her in his arms and strode to the door with her.

"Put me down! This minute, Quinn Mathis!" He loosened his hold and she started to fall. With a strangled cry she flung her arms around his neck and clung to him. "Don't drop me. Don't!" His arms tightened again.

"That's better, my girl. If you struggle, I'll drop you in a gorgeous heap, and we both know you don't want that to happen."

"Where are you taking me?" His nearness sent her senses reeling. What was happening to her? Had she finally met her match? "Where are you taking me?" This time her voice was weak and hoarse.

"Where do you think? To your room. Certainly

not mine. The woman I fall in love with will be soft and feminine and truthful." He started up the stairs, walking easily with her in his arms.

She turned her head with a scowl and her eyes clashed again with his. "I wouldn't fall in love with you if you were the last man on earth. And if you want me to, I'll sign a statement stating that."

He stopped at the top of the stairs and laughed into her flushed face. "You had fun with that at our interview, didn't you? I saw the flash of your eyes and knew that you were angry, but you covered it up and then hit me with all that stuff about signing a paper saying that I didn't have any designs on you."

"You deserved it."

"I didn't deserve the disguise you had on."

"No, no, you didn't. But you wouldn't have given me the job if you'd recognized me."

"You're right about that," he said grimly.

A smile flickered across her face, then she frowned. "Put me down, Quinn. I won't run away."

"You bet you won't!" His arms tightened around her. "I think I'll give Dale Gerard a call and tell him that I tucked his lady into bed. Then we'll see just how long he puts up with you."

He carried her inside her room and with one easy movement tossed her onto the bed. She leaped up. "Get out of my room!"

Without a word he looked around, then scooped up her leather purse, rummaged through it and pulled out her car keys. He tossed them up and caught them with a low laugh. She gasped and lunged at him, grabbing for the keys. With ease he dropped them into his pocket.

She stamped her foot. "Oh! Oh, I have never been so angry in all of my life!"

"I have your keys and that leaves you without a car. I'll tell Barney and Jane that I don't want you driving any of our cars, and you'll be stranded here."

"Why are you doing this to me?"

He leaned over and pushed his face close to hers until his nose almost touched hers. "Nobody does to me what you did and gets by with it. I will not have Yvonne spreading the word that you worked for me without my knowing who and what you were."

"The delicate male ego. Is that why you made me sing with you at the picnic? Is that why you kissed me?"

"Do you call that a kiss? That was a mere peck to make it look like we were very friendly." He laughed gruffly. "If you call that a kiss, then no wonder you can't get poor Dale to the altar."

"You . . . you . . .!"

His long arm snaked around her narrow waist and pulled her against him. Her heart thudded as he lowered his face until his lips touched hers. She struggled, but he pressed his hand against the back of her head so that she couldn't move. His kiss sent sparks shooting along every nerve ending. She gripped his jacket lapels to keep from falling and her eyelids closed. Her will to resist vanished. She slipped her arms up, up around his neck and pushed her fingers through the dark thickness of his hair.

Abruptly he broke from her, his eyes dark with emotion, his face flushed. "That is a kiss, Molly DuPree," he said in a hoarse whisper. He spun on his heels and strode to the door and out.

Molly heard his steps on the stairs. Weakly she sank to the soft carpet with her arms wrapped around herself and rocked back and forth. Her lips tingled and she could still feel the pressure of his arms around her and his kiss that shook her to the very core of her being.

Slowly, her legs trembling, she stumbled to the door, pushing it shut with a sharp snap and locking it. With a shiver she leaned against it and gingerly rubbed her lips with the tips of her fingers. Why had the kiss affected her that way? The light passion that she felt when Dale kissed her was nothing compared to this. What could it mean? Numbly she shook her head.

In a daze she unpacked her bags, unaware that she pushed her clothes in tangled heaps into the drawers. She dropped onto the bed and stared up at the ceiling. The clock ticked in a steady rhythm with her heart. A dog barked in the distance, increasing the sudden loneliness that pressed against her, adding yet another weight to her troubled spirit.

Giant tears welled up in her eyes and slipped down the side of her face. Why had she enjoyed his kiss? Her mind leaped away from the question and even from the kiss. Again she heard the accusations that he'd flung at her in his study. Why didn't she answer him so that he was forced to back down from her? Every word, every inflection of his voice rushed back to her, unreeling in her mind over and over. With a muffled sob she flipped over and buried her face in the pillow. Great racking sobs tore at her throat, and she pressed her face tightly into the pillow so that no sound could seep under her door.

He was right about her. Somewhere along the way she'd compromised her standards. Guilt swamped her and she sobbed harder.

"Oh, God, what have I done?" The words burst from her, burning her throat.

What had happened to her total commitment to Christ? When had she slipped so far away from

Him, from what she knew to be right and true?

"Oh, Heavenly Father, forgive me. I am sorry! So sorry! I was wrong. I need You to guide my life. I love You and I'm thankful for Your love to me. Cleanse my heart and make me pure in Your sight. Help me to know what to do to make right the wrongs I've done." She prayed softly until the burden of guilt and shame lifted and a peace filled her heart.

Several minutes later she sat up, wiped away her tears, and sighed heavily. Somehow she had to put aside her own desires to meet the needs of this family. She had to keep her word to Quinn and stay with the girls for the full six months no matter what became of her job.

Could she do it?

With icy hands she lifted her robe off the foot of the bed and slipped it on. She had promised to take care of the girls for six months and that's just what she would do. But she would not give up the investigation of the accident or the money embezzled from Ardetts. If Amber would allow it, she could work with her to solve the case even if she wasn't able to use the story.

A great peace settled over her and she smiled as she walked across the hall to check the girls. The door was open wider than usual and she frowned. A shiver ran down her spine and she rushed inside. Deanie's bed was empty. Molly gasped, her hand fluttering to her throat. Tonya slept soundly, curled in a tight ball. Molly pulled the sheet up to Tonya's neck, then ran to the bathroom. It was empty.

"Deanie, where are you?"

Molly rushed down the hall, looking in each room. At Quinn's room, she hesitated. What would he think if she knocked on his door this time of night? She frowned. There wasn't time to think of that now.

She knocked on the door, pushing it open a bit. With her heart in her mouth she pushed it open farther and peeked inside. The light from the hall shone across the empty bed and she sighed in relief. She turned to leave, then turned back to study the massive walnut furniture and the brown tones of the room. Shivers ran up and down her spine and color stained her cheeks. A suit coat hung over the back of a chair and shoes stood on the carpet beside the closed closet doors. A tie lay in a heap on the striped bedspread.

What was she doing?

She whirled and ran away from Quinn's bedroom and down the stairs. Suddenly she stopped in mid-stride. Soft music came from the study. Couldn't he sleep either? She flushed and forced back thoughts of his kiss.

The study door stood partly open and she slipped inside, then stopped short. Quinn sat in his chair with Deanie curled on his lap, her head against his chest. They were both sound asleep. Molly stepped forward. A tender feeling swept over her leaving her almost too weak to stand.

She knelt beside the chair and touched Quinn's arm. The feel of his white shirt and muscled arm sent chills over her. His soft breathing blended with Deanie's. Dark lashes rested lightly against sun-browned skin. His usually well-groomed hair was mussed and she wanted to run her fingers through it. Abruptly she pulled away.

"Quinn."

He didn't move.

"Quinn, wake up," she whispered.

His lashes fluttered. He looked directly into her

blue eyes and her heart jerked, then hammered loudly.

"Molly?" He spoke her name just above a whisper. Flames leaped in his eyes, taking her breath away. "Molly!" He sat up with a start, his arms tightening around Deanie. "Is something wrong?"

She wanted to stand, not kneel beside him, but her legs were too weak. "I was looking for Deanie."

He rubbed his cheek against Deanie's soft hair. "I heard her crying when I left your room and I carried her down here to calm her. I guess I fell asleep."

"I hated to wake you, but I thought it would be better."

He smiled and it shot to her heart, startling her with the strange feeling that swept over her. Awkwardly she pushed herself up and forced back the desire to rest her head on his shoulder.

He stood up with Deanie high in his arms. "I'm glad you woke me, Molly. Any longer in that position and I wouldn't have been able to walk." He talked to her as if nothing had happened between them earlier and she was relieved.

"I think Deanie will be all right now." Molly walked beside Quinn up the steps to the bedroom. She pulled back the sheet and blanket and Quinn carefully laid Deanie down, then Molly covered her. Quinn kissed Deanie's soft cheek. Molly followed him into the hall.

"Quinn."

He stopped, his brow cocked questioningly.

She swallowed hard. "I just want you to know that I won't fight you. I'll stay my full time with the girls."

He stood before her, his shirttail hanging over his trousers, the sleeves rolled almost to his elbows, his hands resting lightly on his lean hips. "Well, well."

She forced back a flush. "I was wrong to promise

and then try to break my promise. I was wrong about a lot of things and I'm very sorry."

"Hummm."

"Is that all you can say?"

"I'm speechless. And I'm wondering what game you're playing this time."

"No game." She lifted her chin and met his eyes. "I'm very serious."

"What about your job?"

"I'll manage both."

"And if you can't, Molly?"

She took a deep breath. "The girls do come first for now."

His eyes narrowed. "My, my. It's amazing what a simple kiss will do."

Her temper shot through the ceiling and she glared at him. "There was nothing simple about that kiss and you know it! And I am not staying because of that. I know how wrong I've been. God has forgiven me and I hope you will too. Even if you don't, I'm staying with the girls. If you want, we can manage to avoid each other."

"Nice little speech. I'll have to wait and see if you mean it, won't I? No one cons me the second time around."

"Think what you will." She sailed into her room, but before she closed the door, he blocked the way. She waited, barely breathing.

"I really am amazed at the power of one kiss from me."

She doubled her fists and glared at him.

He threw back his head and laughed, then closed her door and left her alone with her breast rising and falling in agitation.

Impatiently she slipped into her pajamas, clicked off her light and slipped into bed. "I will not be angry at him. I will not be angry at him!"

Slowly she relaxed and sank deeper into the bed, finally closing her eyes. Immediately she felt his arms around her, his lips on hers, and her eyes shot open.

"I won't think about it," she muttered. "The kiss was nothing to me. Nothing!"

She turned on her side and pulled her knees almost to her chin, closed her eyes and finally slept.

Chapter 10

Molly's heels clicked on the sidewalk as she hurried toward Wilkens' Appliances. George Bailer had insisted that she talk to Al again even though she told him that she wouldn't. George said that Al Wilkens was hiding something about the night of the break-in and she was to find out what she could. Molly sighed. She'd talk to Al Wilkens first, then go to Ardetts and see Dale even though he was always busy on Friday. Today Mrs. Mathis had taken the girls shopping and Molly had the day to herself. She needed the time off to give her a chance to think clearly. For the past few days Quinn had acted as if nothing had happened between them. He didn't tell his mother about Molly and she was thankful for that. He explained that she really didn't need to know since she was soon going back to the Lansing store.

Molly had reported almost everything to Amber.

"Thanks for not giving me away," Amber said.

"Why can't you tell me who hired you?"

"I will when I can," Amber replied. Mrs. Mathis still wanted to keep her part in the investigation a secret.

"If we all worked together, maybe we could solve this faster," Molly had said. But Amber wouldn't tell Molly anything more.

"Amber, I'm still going to find answers," Molly muttered as she walked past the cafe. She glanced at her watch. She could catch Dale before he went to lunch if she hurried. For some reason he was avoiding her. He barely talked to her on the phone except for a quick hello and a comment on the weather. Rain spattered against the sidewalk and drizzled down to dampen her hair, curling it even tighter. Stopping outside the appliance store, she saw Billie Lane, the waitress from next door, struggling with Al Wilkens. Angrily Molly burst into the store, the bell tinkling.

"Get your hands off her, Mr. Wilkens!"

He turned with a scowl and Billie Lane pulled free and ran to Molly with tears streaming down her pale face.

"Did he hurt you, Billie?"

"No." Billie trembled as she clasped Molly's arm. "I'm so glad you came in!"

Al Wilkens puffed out his broad chest and strutted forward. He shook his thick finger at Molly. "You get out of here. You're not welcome in my place."

"I don't care to be here, Mr. Wilkens, but I thought the readers would like to know about your latest actions toward a minor. Along with the speculation on your break-in, it should cause quite a stir."

His face turned brick-red and he licked his mustache, then wiped it off. "There's no truth to the story that men were gambling here that night. It's not legal and I don't do anything that's illegal."

"Tell me another story, Mr. Wilkens. I just now saw you trying to force yourself on this minor."

He bristled. "I wasn't doing anything that she didn't want!"

"I didn't want him to touch me or kiss me,"

whispered Billie, clinging to Molly. "I was fired from my other job and I've been working here for a week. I didn't know he wanted me to do anything but wait on customers."

"You can't tell me that, little girl. I made it very plain."

Molly pulled free of Billie and stepped close to Al Wilkens. "She is seventeen years old! She needs a job, but she doesn't need one badly enough to work for a creep like you."

"You think you got all the answers, don't you, curly? I happen to know the little girl will stay here with me." He hiked up his plaid slacks and stood with his feet apart, his cold eyes on Molly. "Now, get out of here."

"What about it, Billie?"

"I need this job, Molly." Her eyes were wide in her pale face and she trembled. She wore blue slacks and a lighter blue knit shirt with a scoop neck. Her hand fluttered to her throat.

Mr. Wilkens reached out his large beefy hand and curled his thick fingers around Billie's thin arm and smirked at Molly. He licked his mustache. "You run along and save them that wants saved."

Molly doubled her fists, spots of bright red on her cheeks. "Billie, you come with me. I'll find you another job."

Al Wilkens clenched and unclenched his hands. "Get out of my store, Molly DuPree. I have every right to refuse service to any customer."

"I am not a customer and I'll never be a customer."

"Please, Molly, just go. I'll finish out the day or he won't pay me." Billie nervously twisted a strand of brown hair.

Al Wilkens jabbed a finger against Billie's thin arm. "You go pull yourself together and comb your hair before a customer comes in."

Billie looked helplessly at Molly, then scurried away with her head down. The restroom door slammed, then all was quiet except for Al Wilkens' wheezing chuckle as he stepped closer to Molly.

Molly backed away, her purse clutched tightly to her. She hated the look in his eyes and knew that if she tried to run past him to the door, he'd grab her and pull her back. He was much stronger than she, even with the tricks her dad had showed her. Her sea-green slacks brushed against a microwave oven on a swivel stand. "Stay away from me, Mr. Wilkens, or I'll scream. Anyone walking past on the sidewalk will come in to see what's happening. You wouldn't want that embarrassment, would you?"

"No one would bother coming in here. Nobody cares." He chuckled wickedly, his eyes almost disappearing from sight in his round face. "You think you're too good for me, don't you, Molly DuPree? You and your important job. Now, you waltz in here on an errand of mercy only to find you are the one who needs help."

She darted a look around for a weapon of some kind. Could she reach the waffle iron and bop him over the head? Silently she prayed for help as she grabbed for the black handle. Before her hand touched it, he clasped his hands around her narrow waist and pulled her to him. She screamed and kicked at him but missed. He laughed.

The bell tinkled and suddenly someone pulled Al Wilkens away from her. She looked up to find Quinn Mathis angrily jerk Al Wilkens across the room. Quinn shoved the startled man down into a chair, then stood over him, his face dark with rage. "Never, never lay a finger on Molly again! If you even speak to her you'll have to answer to me."

Molly brushed tears of relief from her eyes and bit her lower lip as she leaned weakly against the counter. Quinn turned to her and she smiled shakily. He strode to her and slipped an arm around her shoulders. She leaned against him, savoring his strength and the special aroma that belonged only to him.

"Are you all right? Did he hurt you?" His voice was hoarse and she felt him tremble.

A strange weakness swept over her and she gripped the lapel of his jacket. "I'm fine now. Thanks."

Just then Billie stepped out of the restroom, her hand pressed to her heart. "Oh, Molly, I'm sorry that I couldn't help you. I was too scared! Are you sure you're all right?"

She nodded with a shiver.

Billie lifted wide eyes to Quinn. "She came in to help me and he got mean to her. It's all my fault."

"It's over now, Billie." Molly pulled away from Quinn to slip an arm around Billie. "But you can't go on working for him after today. It's not safe."

Quinn shook his head. "No, you certainly will not work another second for this scum. I'll find a job for you."

"Are you sure?"

Molly smiled. "He's a man of his word, Billie. You can trust him." Molly met Quinn's eyes and something flickered for a moment in his, then was gone.

Billie dashed behind the counter and grabbed her purse. "I don't know how I'll ever thank you."

"It's not necessary."

"Or you, Molly. Thank you."

"Billie, you can work for me at my house later today if you want. Cleaning and helping with my nieces," said Quinn as he handed her his card.

Molly bit her lower lip. Maybe Quinn thought he had a way to get rid of her by hiring Billie.

"I'll be there!" Billie squeezed Molly's hand, then ran from the store, the bell tinkling after her.

Quinn walked to Al Wilkens and stood over him. "If you try another trick like that, Mister, you'll be drummed out of business."

"You think you're some hot-shot, don't you, Mr. Mathis? Well, you're not! You and your brother both. He wasn't so special."

Molly took a deep breath. "Was he ever in here when gambling went on?" She felt Quinn jerk, but she didn't take her eyes off Al Wilkens.

"I'm not talking to you about anything."

"Did he know about the gambling?"

Al Wilkens rubbed his damp face. "What gambling?"

"The illegal gambling that went on in your back room," snapped Quinn. "I was coming here to talk to you about that. Now, tell me! Was my brother here trying to stop the gambling?"

"Ha!" Al Wilkens pushed himself up and shoved his hands into his pockets. "Your brother came to play. Why should he break us up? He was in on the whole thing from the beginning."

Molly watched the color drain from Quinn's face. She slipped her hand through his arm to show him her support.

"Steve didn't gamble," said Quinn gruffly.

Al Wilkens laughed. "Didn't he? Ask a few of his friends there at that fancy store of yours. They know. His wife knew."

With a groan Quinn strode out the door with Molly running to keep up with him. He stopped at the edge of the parking lot, his face ashen and his shoulders bent dejectedly. Light drops of rain fell on them unnoticed.

"Quinn, don't take Wilkens' word on this. You know he would lie just to hurt you. You knew your brother and would be aware of something like that." She caught his hand and he didn't pull away. "Don't listen to Wilkens."

"I suppose I am afraid that it could be true. Something was going on with Steve and he wouldn't talk about it."

"Maybe you'll never know. But I think you should believe the best about your brother."

Quinn nodded and squeezed her hand. "Thanks. You're right, Molly. I'll do what I can to learn the truth since it looks like it's connected with his death."

"In what way?"

He looked at her and his face closed as he pulled his hand free. "I won't discuss it with you."

Just then lightning flashed, thunder cracked and a strong wind blew against them.

"Let's go! It's going to pour." He ran with her, then pushed her into his car just as large drops of rain fell from the sky. Rain lashed against the windows. Molly huddled in the passenger seat of the Cadillac. The smell of leather rose around her along with the faint aroma of Quinn's aftershave.

"Two rescues in one day," she said with a breathless laugh. "What more could a girl want?"

"I wonder." His face was thoughtful as he tugged his blue and red striped tie loose and unbuttoned the top button of his white shirt.

She leaned against the door, watching him closely. "One of these days you'll learn to trust me, Quinn."

"Oh? Will I?"

She nodded. She wanted to ask him about the connection between Al Wilkens, Steve and the break-in, but she knew he wouldn't discuss it with her. Maybe there wasn't a connection after all.

"Where are you heading now, Molly?"

"To Ardetts."

"To see me?"

"No. Dale."

He stiffened and tension crackled in the car. "I didn't save you from one man just to toss you to another."

"Don't be ridiculous! Dale and I are going to be married."

"Oh? From my observation he doesn't seem very interested."

She turned to stare out the window. "We've both been very busy."

"Is that so." It was a statement, not a question.

She turned to face him, sparks flying from her eyes. "You should know! The last three nights I helped you with the Boys' Club campout. I've also spent extra time with the girls to leave you free to run around with Yvonne Stoddard!"

"I told you not to be jealous of her."

"I am *not* jealous!" She gripped her purse in her lap so tightly her fingers hurt.

"You're not?"

The look in his eyes and the sound of his husky voice melted her anger. He reached for her and she was powerless to resist. He pulled her close and touched his lips to hers. Sparks flew. Shivers ran over her. A low moan escaped her and her hands slid up and around his neck. The kiss went on until she thought she was drowning. Finally he lifted his head.

"My, my," he said hoarsely. "It's as explosive as I remember."

"Is it?" she whispered, offering her lips again.

Abruptly he pulled away and she watched him, her eyes wide and her heart racing.

"The sooner you get to Dale and talk him into marrying you, the better off we'll all be."

She fumbled with the door handle and slipped from the car, her face hot then cold. Without a backward look she ran through the rain to her yellow Mustang. She slumped down in the seat, trembling. He had kissed her, and she had begged for more! How could she face him again?

Why should his kisses set her on fire this way? She touched her lips and closed her eyes with a soft moan. What was wrong with her? How could she be in love with Dale and still respond in such a way to Quinn?

Impatiently she started the car and drove the several blocks to Ardetts. She had to see Dale now and get it settled with him. They must get married. It was too dangerous to wait another day. She frowned. What a strange thought. Dangerous wasn't the right word. She dealt in words but she still couldn't find a more suitable word.

Several minutes later she stepped out of the elevator and walked into the aisle where the china was on display. A delicate flower pattern caught her attention and she imagined how it would look on her table. But the table she saw in her mind's eye was the table in Quinn's dining room.

She sped past the china as if someone was chasing her. After she talked to Dale, she'd be all right.

Several women and two teenage girls walked around the household items, talking and exclaiming over what they saw. A few feet away Nora Bates waited on a white-haired woman. Dale stood near the cash register, watching Nora with an open admiration and pride that startled Molly. What was going on between Dale and Nora? Molly frowned. She would not allow her vivid imagination to get away from her.

"Hello, Dale." She smiled and touched his arm.

His eyes widened and he shot a look to Nora before he gave Molly his full attention. "Hi. I didn't know you were coming in today. I thought Mr. Mathis had you tied down at his place."

"I hope you're not still angry that I'm working for him. I told you why. You said that it was all right with you. Remember?"

"I remember. I just don't know if I'll ever get used to you and your crazy tricks."

"Oh, Dale." She laughed softly and stepped closer to him, but he jerked back with another look at Nora. Molly pretended not to notice. "Let's have lunch today and catch up with each other. It's been a long time."

"You know we're busy." Dale pushed his fingers through his blond hair, then rubbed it flat again.

She nodded, surprised that she wasn't disappointed. That disturbed her and she caught his hand and clung to it. "Please, Dale. We haven't had any time together for a long time. Take off an hour, please. Half hour? Oh, please, Dale!"

He shook his head and glanced at Nora, then back to Molly. "But we must talk soon, Molly. I'll come to the Mathis's and we'll find a spot to be alone and talk. I'm sure Mr. Mathis won't object as long as I don't stay long."

"Can't you take time now?"

Nora had stepped close enough to hear. She smiled at Molly, then turned wide eyes on Dale. "I can surely take care of things for a while, Dale. You go ahead with Molly and talk to her."

Dale sighed, glanced at his watch, then nodded. "Maybe this is for the best." He ran his finger around the inside of his pale yellow shirt collar and looked helplessly at Nora. She smiled and he squared his wide shoulders. "We'll go to the coffee shop next door, but we can't stay long."

"All right." Molly saw the look that passed between Dale and Nora and it troubled her, but she didn't say anything as she walked with Dale to the elevator. She slipped her hand through his arm and felt him stiffen. He moved away as he pressed the down button and her hand dropped to her side. She left it there. Something was wrong and soon she would know what it was.

Several people shared the elevator, making it impossible to talk. Molly stood close to Dale, her eyes glued to the doors. He seemed cold and distant and it disturbed her. Even more disturbing was the fact that her mind kept drifting to Quinn so that Dale seemed just one of the strangers sharing the ride.

The doors slid open and Quinn stepped inside. He seemed to fill the space. He stopped, his eyes riveted to hers, then he looked coldly at Dale. Dale smiled hesitantly and Molly struggled to keep her hands from trembling and her heart from leaping. She lowered her eyes to hide any telltale secrets only to find herself looking at Quinn's highly polished black shoes. Just yesterday she'd helped the girls polish them for him.

Again the elevator stopped and when the doors closed only Molly, Dale and Quinn stood inside the small enclosure. The soft whirr of the elevator and her own wild heartbeats were the only sounds she heard. Smells of perfume and lotion and tobacco lingered in the air.

Dale cleared his throat.

Quinn said, "Taking time off, Dale?"

"Yes, Mr. Mathis. Only a few minutes. I trust you don't mind."

Molly glanced up at Quinn, her face masked,

then glanced away when her eyes clashed with his.

"But I do mind, Dale. We're busy. Conduct your personal life after hours." He folded his arms across his chest and the tan jacket tightened across his back and shoulders.

"You're right, Mr. Mathis," Dale said meekly.

Molly's anger flared and she gripped her purse tighter. "We're going to the coffee shop for a few minutes, Quinn. I'm sure you won't lose money if Dale's gone for a short while."

"Molly!" Dale nudged her and shook his head. "I'm sorry, Mr. Mathis. Molly doesn't know the policy. I wanted a chance to speak with her and I didn't think it could wait."

Quinn eyed him coldly. "And now?"

The elevator stopped on the ground floor but no one made a move to step out. No passenger waited to enter. Molly looked from Quinn's set face to Dale's apologetic one. "Don't let him bully you, Dale."

Dale flushed. "Molly!" He turned to Quinn. "I'll get back to work. Molly and I can talk one of these evenings at your home."

Quinn cleared his throat. "I don't think that's wise."

"We'll work something out," said Dale stiffly while Molly fumed. Dale made a move to step out, but Quinn blocked the door and Dale was forced to stop.

"If you need a few minutes and want privacy, you can use my office. I'll ride up with you and tell my secretary." Quinn didn't wait for an answer, but jabbed the button and the doors closed. He moved until he stood beside Molly, his arms crossed and his aftershave tickling her nose. She bit her tongue to keep back a sharp retort as she stepped closer to Dale. Quinn glanced at her then away. Tension crackled in the air and Molly shivered. The swift rise to the top floor made her momentarily dizzy.

"This really isn't necessary," said Dale weakly.

Finally the doors opened and Quinn led the way to his office. He opened his door and stepped aside. "Molly, I'd like a word with you when Dale is finished. I'll wait with Mary."

Dale tugged at his collar. "We don't want to keep you from your office, Mr. Mathis. We can talk another time."

"Why wait? Go right in and make yourselves comfortable."

Molly sailed past Quinn and stopped in the middle of the spacious room. She hadn't been back since her job interview and she felt slightly uncomfortable. When the door clicked shut behind Quinn she turned to frown at Dale. "You shouldn't let him run over you that way. You aren't a slave, you know."

"I can't afford to lose my job, Molly." Dale dabbed his forehead with a white handkerchief, then pushed it back into his pocket.

"But you don't have to be a doormat!"

"Let's drop it, Molly!" Dale's blue eyes were icy. "I have something very important to say to you and I don't want to wait any longer to say it. Just keep quiet until I've finished. Please."

She frowned as she sank back against Quinn's large desk. How determined Dale looked! She watched as he paced the room, then stopped in front of her, a strained look on his face.

"Molly, I don't want to hurt you but—it's over between us."

"What?" Had she heard correctly?

"I mean it, Molly. We're not right for each other. We don't even love each other."

"You can't mean what you're saying, Dale! We've been in love for ages!" She reached for his hands, but he drew back. "We have!"

"Molly, I'm in love with someone else. Really in love. It was love at first sight almost. I can't live without her."

"Oh!" Molly pressed her hands to her burning cheeks.

"Don't look like that, Molly. You must realize that our love wasn't a strong, passionate love."

She shook her head, unable to think straight.

"You'll find someone to love, Molly."

"But I love you!"

"You don't really love me, not the way Nora does."

"Nora?" She whispered the name through an aching throat.

"Nora Bates. It was love at first sight, but neither one of us wanted to admit it until we couldn't deny it any longer."

"Nora Bates? The little girl from Montana?"

He nodded as he straightened his tie. "She loves me the way I am."

"I do too!"

"No. No, Molly, you always wanted to change me."

She flushed as she realized it was true.

"I don't want to hurt you, but you must know. I wanted to tell you at the picnic, but I didn't know how."

"I must be having a bad dream." Pain squeezed her heart and she wanted to cry out in agony.

Dale moved uneasily. "We're getting married soon."

"Oh, my! Married soon."

Dale cleared his throat. "That's what I wanted to

say. I'd better get back to work. You can keep the bracelet I gave you for Christmas."

She sank to the couch and watched through a blur of tears as he walked out. Quinn stepped into the room and closed the door with a bang. She lowered her head, but not before he saw the tears. She rubbed her eyes to stop the flow but it didn't help.

He sat beside her. "What happened?" She wouldn't look at him. "Tell me, Molly."

More tears welled up and spilled out and she sniffed as she tried to speak.

He slipped strong, comforting arms around her and pulled her close to his chest. She stiffened, then leaned against him with her face pressed into his white shirt. A sob tore from her, then another. With a shudder she clung to him, sobbing out her heartbreak. He held her without speaking and rubbed her back soothingly. She could feel his heart thud against her ear. The realization that she was in his arms dried her tears instantly. She drew away and he let her go. He pushed a handkerchief into her hands and she wiped her eyes and blew her nose.

"He ... aw ... he is going to ... to marry ... marry Nora ... Bates."

"Is he now?"

"I love him." Her breast rose and fell as she crushed the hanky in her hand. "I have loved him for so long!"

Quinn stood in one fluid movement. His shirt-sleeves were rolled up on his strong, brown arms. "Stop lying to yourself, Molly!"

"What?"

"You heard me."

"I do love him!"

"You don't love Dale Gerard, Molly."

"How can you say that?" she asked in a weak voice.

"If you did, you wouldn't be sending me the vibes you've been sending me since the day we met."

"What?" Her voice rose into a shriek and she leaped up, flags of red flying in her cheeks and fire blazing from her eyes.

"You said that there was no way you'd fall in love with me."

"Stop it!"

"You gave your word, but I think it's just another time when your word means nothing to you."

Words failed her and she sputtered, her fists doubled.

He stepped close to her. "You love me. Admit it, Molly DuPree."

"What? How arrogant!"

"You would jump at the chance to marry me."

"I have never been so ... so ... I wouldn't fall in love with you if ... Right at this moment I don't even like you!"

Pain flashed in his eyes, then was gone. She didn't know if she'd even seen it clearly in her agitated state. He smiled lazily. "Are you expecting me to chase you until suddenly you turn and catch me?"

"What? Oh, I've never ..."

"I'm a good catch. You said so yourself."

She stamped her foot and strode to the door, then whirled around to face him again. "Why are you saying these things to me? Why?"

He crossed his arms and smiled slightly. "To clear the air. You work for me, Molly. I can't have you suddenly falling all over me with a declaration of undying love."

"You ... you ..."

"Have I left you speechless again?"

She stepped toward him, then stopped to face him squarely in all her blazing glory. "Fire me, Quinn, if that's the way you feel. I don't need the job, you know. I am only staying because of the girls."

"I just wanted you to know that I know of your attraction for me. Even Yvonne Stoddard noticed and commented on it."

She threw up her arms. "I can't believe what I'm hearing! I'm going home."

"Yours or mine?"

Sparks flew from her sapphire eyes. "Yours, of course. Isn't that where you insisted I live?"

She saw the twinkle in his eye and she stopped. He eyes grew big and round. She shook her finger under his nose. "You have been goading me. Teasing me."

"You're right."

"Why?"

He grinned and bobbed his dark brows.

"How could you be so cruel?"

He tapped the end of her nose. "I made you forget the broken heart you were so determined to have."

She pressed her hands to her burning cheeks.

"You don't care two cents' worth for that man or the little girl from Montana."

"Oh!"

"Admit it."

She searched her heart and discovered to her chagrin that he was right, but she didn't like the smug look on Quinn's face. Mischief glinted in her eyes and she quickly masked it as she stepped close to him. "You could be right, Quinn. I just wish I had a way to know the truth."

"You do know the truth," he said sharply, looking at her quizzically.

"Dale's kisses thrilled me and made me feel in love. But Quinn, it's strange, but your kisses thrilled me too."

He frowned, shifting restlessly.

"Do you think it's possible that I don't even know what love is?"

"I told you once that you didn't."

"You could be right." She frowned thoughtfully and tapped her finger on her chin. "I wonder if I should stop a total stranger and ask him to kiss me so that I can compare my feelings?"

"Molly!"

She stepped right up to him. "What do you think?"

"That's enough, Molly. Run on home and tell Jane that Yvonne will be there for dinner."

A shaft of jealousy ripped through her, but she waved her hand and flipped back her hair. "Who needs love? When I want that special feeling, that thrill, I'll just come to you for a few wonderful kisses."

He pointed to the door. "Go!"

"See you at home." She lifted her hand and sailed from the room with a bright laugh. Once in the elevator she sagged weakly against the bar, closed her eyes, and tried to stop the wild beating of her heart.

Chapter 11

Amber reached across the kitchen table and touched Molly's hand. "You know the Bible says you must forgive Dale."

"Well, I won't!"

"You're better off without him, Molly. God has someone else for you."

"But we've been going together for a long, long time!"

"You must face the truth, Molly. I know I'm repeating what I said the other day when you first told me about you and Dale breaking up, but I believe it with all my heart. Only your pride is hurt and not your heart at all. I've known for a while that you and Dale didn't love each other. You know it, too, but you're too stubborn to admit it."

"But Amber, it hurts so much!"

"It's the end of a dream, Molly. Now get on with your life. Forgive Dale and the pain will go away. You're angry at him for hurting you." Amber thought about her struggle to forgive Dad and the anguish she went through. "Don't hold on to that anger or the pain will stay. God has promised to help you forgive."

"I can't forgive him! He hurt me deeply. He's going to marry Nora Bates!" She pushed aside her teacup and saucer. "It's asking too much to forgive and forget. I've been humiliated in front of all the people I've told that we were planning to marry."

Amber shook her head. "Molly, you're only hurting yourself if you don't forgive. It'll eat away inside you."

"I don't care!" She jumped up. "I have to get the girls and go outdoors to help get ready for those boys."

"It was nice of Quinn to let ten more boys camp out here when he learned that Henry Black couldn't take them. Quinn's a wonderful man."

Molly's throat closed over and she walked out. She forced her weak legs to carry her upstairs. In the hallway she heard shrill angry voices coming from the girls' room. Molly hurried to the doorway. "Girls! What's going on?"

Deanie turned an angry face toward Molly. "I hate Tonya! I don't want her for a sister any more!"

Tears spilled down Tonya's pale face. "I didn't mean to break it, Deanie. I was only looking at it and it fell and broke."

Molly stepped into the room.

"She did that!" Deanie pointed a shaking finger at her latest prize possession, a blown glass unicorn with a blue horn. A horse lay on the desk next to the broken unicorn. "I told her not to touch it ever! I told her it would break!"

"I didn't mean to do it." Tonya covered her face with trembling hands and sobbed harder.

Molly pulled Tonya close, then reached for Deanie's hand. Deanie jumped back, a stubborn look on her small face. Her long red hair hung in tangles.

"Deanie, I'll see if I can glue the unicorn back together. If I can't, I'll buy a new one."

"I want this one!" She crossed her arms over her thin chest and poked out her bottom lip.

Molly sat on the edge of Deanie's bed, her arm around Tonya's small body. "Deanie, you know Tonya is sorry. Can't you forgive her and enjoy the day that's ahead?" The words mocked her and she knew she had no right to say them to anyone.

"I'll never forgive her!" Deanie turned away. "I'm going to stay away from her and never play with her again!"

Tonya sobbed harder and Molly sighed helplessly. The unicorn was broken. It had probably meant more to Deanie than Dale had to her.

She sucked in her breath at the terrible thought. She did love Dale! He couldn't be replaced the way a unicorn could.

At a sound in the doorway she looked up and saw Quinn. Her heart lurched and her nerves tingled. He wore faded blue cut-offs and a blue and white tee shirt that showed off the muscles in his arms and across his chest.

"What's going on up here?" He looked at her then quickly looked away. She felt as if all the air had gone out of her. Lately he stayed away from her as much as she avoided him.

Tonya ran to him and he lifted her high, only to have Deanie cling to his arm. Both girls talked at once. Finally he sat on a chair and pulled both girls onto his lap, one on each knee. Molly sank to the bed and hugged a stuffed rabbit. If she tried to walk out, she might fall and really embarrass herself.

Quinn kissed Deanie's flushed cheek, then Tonya's pale one. "Deanie, let's talk about forgiving Tonya."

"No!" Deanie shook her head and her hair whipped against Quinn.

Molly sat very still, barely breathing.

"We must," said Quinn firmly. "If you stay angry at Tonya, it'll hurt you and Tonya and even all of us around you."

"I don't care!"

"I know better." He pulled her closer and she finally rested her head against him. Tonya sat very erect, her tears drying on her face. "If you continue to be angry it's like having a black sick spot inside you. It touches other places in you and makes them black and sick and before you know it, your anger rules you. If that happens then it leaves no place for God. He knows unforgiveness is dangerous to you, so he tells us to forgive. You'd be worse off than your unicorn if you continued to be angry at your sister. It hurts you and her and all of us."

Molly suddenly saw the damage she was doing to herself and the others around her because she wouldn't forgive. Tears of remorse burned her eyes. The anger she felt had spilled over to this household and was affecting everyone. With a sniff she ran from the room and across the hall to hers. She closed the door with a sharp snap, then leaned against it, tears sliding down her pale cheeks.

"Heavenly Father, I am sorry for holding on to my anger at Dale. I forgive him for the pain he caused me and the humiliation.

Take away the pain and loss that I feel and help me to be loving and kind to people around me. Help me to be loving and kind even if I never fall in love and marry." Maybe she'd be like little Miss Collins at church and do good works and have a career, but no private love life and no family.

Molly sniffed and wiped her eyes and blew her nose. It was time to put Dale in her past and leave him there. To tell the truth, her pride really was hurt more than her heart. She sniffed again and rubbed her warm cheeks. "Father God, I want what You want for my life. Help me to know what it is and then follow it."

A deep peace settled over her and she smiled a real smile for the first time in days. Now she could get on with her life. She peeked out into the hall and listened. Quinn and the girls were gone. Before she faced them, she wanted to talk to Amber.

In the kitchen Amber turned from the counter and smiled hesitantly.

Molly smiled and rubbed the belt of her shorts. "You're a good friend and I've been terrible. Forgive me?"

Amber smiled. "Sure. I knew you'd come around. You can't stay down for long, not Molly Lynn DuPree."

"Thanks." Molly told her how she'd come to realize that she had to forgive Dale.

Amber smiled and wiped away a tear.

Molly glanced out the window where the girls were playing with Billie Lane. "Billie really is working out, isn't she? She fits right in."

"I'm glad you got her away from Al Wilkens."

"He's no good." Molly talked a few minutes more with Amber, then walked out into the bright morning sunlight. Birds sang in the trees and a tractor roared in a field across the road. A long white car stood near the garage and Molly frowned. The car belonged to Yvonne Stoddard. It was her new one.

"Just what is she doing here so early?" muttered Molly as she walked slowly toward the back lawn where the tent was pitched. Yvonne stood beside Quinn and the girls.

"Molly!" Deanie ran across the yard to Molly. "Molly, Uncle Quinn said I upset you. Did I?"

Molly knelt in the soft grass and held Deanie close. "No, you didn't. I hurt myself. You see, I couldn't forgive someone who had hurt me. When your uncle talked to you about forgiving, it helped me. I had to be by myself for a while. But now I'm all right. I've been terrible lately and I'm sorry. Will you forgive me?"

"Yes." Deanie smiled and kissed Molly's cheek.

"Just like that?" Molly held Deanie away from her and looked at her smiling face.

Deanie nodded. "Uncle Quinn said that Jesus wants me to forgive, so I do. I forgave Tonya, but she's going to buy me a new unicorn with a blue horn. It won't be the same as mine, but I'll love it anyway."

Molly laughed and kissed Deanie's red cheek. "I love you."

Deanie pulled away with a frown. "That's what Mrs. Stoddard says but she doesn't mean it. She wants Uncle Quinn to look at her and think she's great. She wants to marry him but me and Tonya don't want him to marry her."

Neither did Molly but she didn't say it.

"Me and Tonya want *you* to marry him. We told him."

Molly flushed painfully and she jerked upright. Her heart raced and she could barely breathe.

"Molly, will you marry him?"

She lowered her voice. "Please don't say anything more to your uncle about it."

"Are you mad?"

"No, but I will be if you say anything more. I mean it."

Deanie frowned and shook her head. "Uncle Quinn said the same thing."

"Did he?" Weakness washed over her and she sank to the ground, her face white.

"Don't faint, Molly! Uncle Quinn, Molly's going to faint!"

"I'm all right, Deanie." She tried to stand but her legs wouldn't hold her. Suddenly Quinn's strong arms circled her and lifted her and the thud of her heart almost deafened her.

"Molly, what's wrong? I know you've not been yourself lately. Deanie, tell the others that I'll be out in a few minutes after I take Molly inside."

She tried to pull away but his arms tightened. "I can walk by myself, Quinn. Don't worry about me."

"Why, a strong puff of wind would blow you away. That Dale Gerard has a lot to answer for!"

"I don't understand what happened to me. My legs just wouldn't hold me." She leaned against him as he walked her to the study and sat with her on the couch.

He smoothed her hair back from her face. "I want to make sure that you're not fading away into nothing because of that man. I should fire him!"

"No, no, Quinn. Dale did me a favor, but I just didn't realize it until today. I wasn't really in love with him. My pride was hurt, not my heart."

Quinn lifted his dark brows a fraction and his arm rested heavily on her shoulders. "You were planning to marry the man!"

"I know. I was wrong. I may never marry."

A strange look crossed his face, then was gone. "You still have plenty of time." He hesitated, then stood. "If you don't feel up to helping out, I'm sure Billie will take your place."

"I can manage. I'll be out in a minute."

"Billie fits in quite well here, doesn't she?"

"Yes." Molly settled back on the couch with a grin. "You know she worships you, don't you?"

He grinned and nodded. "I've noticed."

Her eyes twinkled. "Maybe you should have her sign a paper saying that she won't fall in love with you."

He rolled his eyes. "I wish you'd let me forget that."

She chuckled. "I guess I should." She wanted him to sit back down beside her and talk to her longer. "It's so much fun to tease you."

"Yes, well, I suppose I should get going." He looped his thumbs in his pockets, but didn't move.

"It's kind of you to invite more boys to camp out since you already did the group that Steve was to take."

"I couldn't let them be disappointed just because Henry Black couldn't have them. Could I?"

"No. No, you wouldn't. You're a kind, thoughtful man."

He laughed and she saw a pleased look in his eye. "Maybe if I stay here, you'll say more good things about me."

"I might."

"What would you say?"

"What do you want me to say?"

"That I'm handsome, charming, debonair. Shall I go on?" He laughed, and she joined in as she pushed herself up off the couch.

She stood very still, watching him, waiting for something to happen.

He nodded, then stood quietly looking at her. Finally he turned away. "I can't stand here all day, can I? See you later." He turned at the door. "You rest a bit before you come out."

Later she watched Quinn with ten little boys swarming over him in a wrestling match on the grass. He didn't look like the big boss at Ardetts. He didn't seem to have a care in the world, but she knew he was still trying to solve the mystery around Steve's death as well as learn who had taken the money from Ardetts. Today he'd set it aside to give ten boys an enjoyable time.

His booming laugh rang out along with the

giggles and shouts of the boys. Tonya and Deanie stood on the sidelines, watching. Molly knew by the look on Deanie's face that soon she would jump right into the middle of tangled arms and legs.

A sharp tang of perfume stung Molly's nose and she turned her head to see Yvonne beside her.

"You're in love with the man, aren't you?" Yvonne shook her head and sneered. "If he finds out, you'll be out of here faster than you can type an article."

"You can't stand the competition, can you?" Molly stood with her hands on her narrow waist, her elbows jabbing the air.

"What competition is that?" Yvonne lifted her chin and looked down her surgery-perfect nose at Molly.

"Why, the girls and boys, of course. What else could I mean?"

Bright red flags appeared in Yvonne's cheeks and sparks shot from her eyes. "You think you're cute, don't you? You run after Quinn with your heart on your sleeve, waiting for him to notice you, maybe even give you a good story. Well, you might be in love with him, but he isn't with you!"

"Are you sure about that?" Molly knew the truth but she loved to antagonize Yvonne.

"I intend to marry him. You can go play in someone else's yard!"

"But I like this yard." She itched to slap Yvonne and send her flying home. How dare she announce that she was going to marry Quinn?

"It would be a giant step for you to marry into the Mathis family, wouldn't it? A career and a good marriage. But it's not going to happen, Molly DuPree! I'll see to it."

"Pull in your long red nails before you hurt yourself, Yvonne. I think that you're forgetting all the years we've fought, and I've won. You are no match for me and you never will be."

"Oh, how I hate you!"

"Don't waste the energy, Yvonne. Save it to get out of the mess you're in because of Steve Mathis." Molly watched Yvonne closely, hoping for some helpful clue.

Yvonne's face closed and she forced a bright smile. "Always the little reporter, aren't you? You can't trap me into saying anything. Steve was into gambling and I went with him a couple of times just for laughs."

"And did you lose money to Al Wilkens?"

"A little. Who didn't? It was fun while it lasted."

"I hear you were at Ardetts' party with Mark Petersen the night of the accident."

Yvonne's eyes widened and she laughed a brittle laugh. "So what? We're friends."

"How much gambling did Mark do?" Molly used her favorite trick; ask a question as if she knew a fact. She'd never heard Mark's name connected with gambling. She saw the hesitation on Yvonne's face.

"A little. But it's none of your business." She flipped back her blond hair with a shapely hand. "I don't care to talk to you another second. I want you to keep your hands off Quinn or you'll be very sorry."

Molly laughed softly and pushed her face close to Yvonne's. "I will not keep my hands off Quinn Mathis. I will not step aside for you to get your talons in him. You're warning the wrong girl off, and you should know it. Threats *never* work with me."

With an unladylike snort Yvonne spun around and practically ran across the yard toward Quinn and the children.

Molly sucked in air and forced back the anger she

felt toward Yvonne. How dare Yvonne say that she loved Quinn and that Molly should keep away from him?

Did she love him?

Her eyes widened as she stared at him across the yard, her hands locked together to stop their trembling. He stood with a boy on his broad shoulders and another wrapped around his ankle, trying to hold him in place. His hearty laugh boomed out and the sound curled around her heart. A yearning to be near him, to touch him, rose inside her and overwhelmed her. She sank against the giant stone flower pot.

She *did* love him! She did!

But the feeling was nothing like she had felt for Dale. This was a consuming fire that burned inside her. She loved him and her life wouldn't be complete unless he loved her in return.

What would he do if he learned that she had indeed fallen in love with him? Should she leap up on the picnic table and shout it for all to hear? A shaky laugh escaped involuntarily and she shook her head. Maybe she could have it printed in the headlines of the *Freburg News*.

"Oh, Molly, you've done it again," she whispered. This was something she couldn't avoid. Her love for him was sure and nothing would change that. Somehow she would have to keep it hidden from Quinn.

Molly turned toward the house. Right now she needed to be alone to get used to the idea of loving Quinn Mathis. Just as she reached the door Billie shouted to her. She hesitated, then turned with a slight smile.

"Quinn wants you to sing for us now, Molly. The boys love guitar and he said you play beautifully."

With a pleading look on her face, Billie waited for Molly's response.

Molly looked helplessly toward Quinn. How could she sing and play as if nothing unusual had happened? How could she perform when she wanted to shout out the love message of all generations? She imagined Yvonne standing back and laughing as Quinn tossed Molly DuPree out on her ear.

"I'll sing with you if you're scared," said Billie softly.

"Thanks, Billie. I'll get my guitar and be right out."

"Quinn already brought it out. See? He's holding it and waiting for you. He said he'll sing with you."

Her heart lurched. She rubbed her hands down her shorts and took a deep breath. Somehow, she'd have to stand beside him and sing with him.

Molly squared her shoulders and lifted her chin as she walked with Billie toward the waiting group. She greeted the boys and reached out for the guitar without meeting Quinn's eyes.

"Are you all right?" he asked in a low voice for her ears alone.

She nodded, but still couldn't look at him.

"Play a funny song," shouted a red-headed, freckle-faced boy.

"Let her sing what she wants," said Tonya, surprising Molly so much that she looked at Quinn to get his reaction. He smiled and her pulse leaped.

With sparkling eyes and lilting voice Molly sang her first song, a noisy, happy song that pleased everyone except Yvonne who frowned. When Quinn stepped up beside Molly to sing, Yvonne's eyes shot daggers at her. Molly looked right at her and smiled a knowing smile. Yvonne spun around and walked away in a huff. In a few minutes her car shot out of the drive. Laughter bubbled up inside Molly and spilled out right in the middle of the song.

Quinn shot her a questioning look but she shrugged and continued singing. When the singing was finished she stepped away from Quinn and his magnetic personality before he could touch her. This wasn't the place to lose control and fling herself into his arms.

When the boys ran to change into swim trunks Quinn pulled Molly aside.

"I saw you talking with Yvonne. Did you get any information out of her?"

Molly's brain whirled. "Should I have?"

"I can't get anywhere with her. But you can get people to talk even when they don't want to. Just tell me if you learned anything."

"If I do, will you tell me what you already know?"

"No!"

"If we work together on this, maybe we'll get somewhere."

He sighed heavily. "Never mind, Molly. If you won't help me, you won't. Go change into your swimsuit." He sounded depressed and discouraged. She touched his arm. His eyes were guarded as he looked at her.

"Yvonne said that Mark Petersen gambled at Wilkens' too. She went a few times with him and with . . . Steve."

Quinn rubbed a hand over his face.

"Maybe Steve was there to investigate it."

"I'd like to believe that, Molly."

"Trust your heart, Quinn."

His eyes locked with hers. "I don't know if I can."

She trembled but, before she could speak again, the girls shouted for her. "I guess I'd better go change."

He nodded.

Reluctantly she turned away from him and ran to the house. If she looked into his eyes a moment longer, she might get the wild notion that he cared for her, maybe even loved her. She trembled at the thought, but forced it away. She would not let her imagination get away from her this time!

Later the hot sun shone down on her as she stood at the side of the pool watching the boys swim. The girls splashed at the shallow end and Quinn sat on the edge near the deep end. He wore black trunks and had a white towel draped around his neck, making his skin appear darker. The air rang with noise, happy noise that Molly enjoyed hearing. By the smile on Quinn's face she knew he liked it too.

"It never ceases to thrill me, Molly."

She turned to find Mrs. Mathis beside her. "Hello. I didn't know you were coming today."

"It was a last-minute decision. I'm seriously considering joining the children. I'm amazed at the happiness our little campouts bring everyone." She slipped off her light blue jacket and pushed her fingers through her ash-blond hair. "It is hot today."

"The children would love having you swim with them."

"I enjoy the boys. This is the first year that I wasn't here to help with the campout. Steve and Barb had a lot of fun with them, and I see Quinn does too. It's sweet of him to do this twice in one month."

"He's a wonderful man." Molly forced back the flush at Mrs. Mathis's quick look.

"He is that. I'm glad Mrs. Stoddard isn't here today."

"She was, but left. I don't think this is her kind of

thing."

Mrs. Mathis laughed. "No, it isn't. But you seem to enjoy it."

"Yes, I do. I know I'll miss it when I'm gone. Being a reporter is great, but so is this." Molly stopped abruptly, her eyes wide with sudden shock.

Mrs. Mathis laughed and patted Molly's shoulder. "Don't be upset, dear. Amber told me who you really were when you first came."

From behind Molly, Amber said, "I had to tell her."

Molly flushed scarlet.

Smiling, Amber sat beside Mrs. Mathis and set a tray of iced tea on the table. "She's the one who hired me."

Mrs. Mathis nodded. "Molly, I didn't tell Quinn about you because I knew he'd toss you right out. Amber said with your reputation she knew you'd get to the bottom of the mystery and write a truthful account of it."

Amber said, "I thought you and I could learn the truth behind Steve's death, so I suggested she keep the knowledge to herself. Quinn doesn't know about me either."

"No. He would object," said Mrs. Mathis. "He likes things his own way."

"You're right." Molly rubbed a hand over her towel. "I appreciate your trust. Quinn doesn't trust me, though. I'm afraid he can't forget that I deceived him."

Mrs. Mathis took the glass of iced tea that Amber handed her. "Quinn is a fine man, but he does have his faults just as we all do. One of these days he'll realize that he can trust you, and you'll be his friend for life. With Quinn, once a friend, always a friend. My son is very loyal."

Molly wanted Mrs. Mathis to continue, but she was afraid her love for Quinn would show. "What about Steve? What kind of man was he?"

Mrs. Mathis smoothed her folded jacket over her knees. "I'm sure you've heard the rumors. I knew my son very well and I know that he loved Barb and wouldn't do anything to jeopardize his marriage."

"Would he have . . . gambled?" asked Amber.

"No! I would never believe that of him!"

Molly deliberated for a moment, then told Mrs. Mathis all that she'd heard and learned.

Amber kept quiet about the notebook that she had discovered. She leaned forward and said, "I found a note in Steve's things. It was a very abrupt sort of note. It said, 'It's on for tonight at ten. Wilkens' Appliances. Knock three times, then once.' And that's one of the nights he was seen with Yvonne Stoddard."

"I know my son. He wouldn't gamble."

Amber rubbed the condensation on her iced tea glass, but didn't say anything.

Molly nodded. "That's what I told Quinn. He said he wanted to believe it."

"Quinn has been away for several years, and hasn't been as close to Steve as he was in the past when they were in school together. Steve wouldn't gamble. And he would never step out on his wife."

Molly leaned forward. "Quinn should know this. Will you tell him?"

She nodded. "But it'll have to wait until I have his attention after the boys are gone."

Amber pushed herself up. "I'd better get back inside." She had to check in with Mina to see if she'd learned the date of the next secret meeting at Wilkens' Appliances. She picked up the empty glasses and walked away.

Mrs. Mathis stood up and laid her jacket over her arm. "I'll go change and be right back." She turned away, then turned back. "Molly, you're a wonderful girl. You have my blessings."

Molly sat very still. "Oh?"

"I saw your face when you were looking at Quinn, my dear. I know what's in your heart for my son. I've watched the two of you together. You're a fine match for him. He needs a strong woman like you."

Molly pressed her trembling hands to her hot cheeks. "Who else has guessed my secret?"

"You must remember that where my son is concerned, I'm very perceptive and observant." She smiled and walked to the house.

Molly leaped up and spun around colliding with Quinn. A shock passed through her. She mumbled, "Excuse me." ·

Quinn frowned. "Why so jumpy? Did Mother say something to upset you?"

Molly shrugged. "She's going to change and come back to swim with us. Won't the kids love it?"

"Yes." He studied her thoughtfully. "There's something different about you, Molly. I can't put my finger on it, but you have an electricity about you that I can feel, but not understand."

If only he knew! She forced a laugh. "It's your imagination, Quinn. I thought only writers had vivid imaginations."

"Mother told you something that excited you, didn't she? Tell me! What is it?" He leaned down until his breath fanned her face and she resisted the urge to circle his neck with her arms and kiss him.

"You'll have to ask her, Quinn."

"Don't think I won't!" He turned abruptly, ran to the pool and jumped in, splashing water up on the tile.

She laughed breathlessly, then followed him, the cold water closing delightfully over her body.

Little boys swarmed around her and she splashed them and shouted to them, her voice ringing out merrily. Several times she saw Quinn watching her, but he didn't come close enough to talk to her again. She knew that he stayed away on purpose.

Had he guessed her wonderful, beautiful, terrible secret? She shivered and dived under the water out of his sight.

Chapter 12

Sunday morning summer rain streaked the church windows as Amber filed out of the sanctuary into the foyer. People pressed against her, talking and laughing. She spotted Jack and slipped around three men finally reaching his side. "Hi, Jack."

"How's it going, Amber?"

"Slow."

"Tina's getting the baby from the nursery. I told her I wanted to see how you are." Jack grinned and moved aside to let others pass.

"Listen, Jack, Barney told me you checked over Steve Mathis's car the day of the accident and it was in perfect condition. Do you know what happened to the brakes?"

"Somehow the fluid was gone."

"Is it easy to drain out the fluid? Is it something that I could do, or does it take a special knowledge?"

He rubbed his jaw thoughtfully. "That reminds me of something, Amber. A man came in to talk to me about that same thing. I forgot all about that. He asked me and I showed him, but he didn't want his car checked."

"Who was the man?"

"Let me think. I didn't know him, but the kid who worked with me that day did." Jack narrowed his eyes and chewed his bottom lip. "I remember.

Petersen. Mark Petersen."

Amber gasped. "What day did he talk to you, Jack?"

"It was the same day Steve Mathis's car was in. In fact, I showed him the brake-line on Mathis's car."

Amber's pulse raced. "That's very interesting."

"Do you know him?"

Amber nodded. "He works at Ardetts."

"You don't say!"

"Did you mention this to the police?"

"I didn't have any reason to. Besides, it totally slipped my mind until you asked about brake fluid just now."

"Jack, thanks for the info. I'll let you know if anything comes of it." She slipped out the door and dashed through the rain to her car. Her mind raced as she drove to her apartment. Was it a coincidence that Mark asked about the brakes? Dare she drive to his place and talk to him?

Several minutes later she ate a tuna sandwich, drank a glass of water and fixed a hot fudge sundae covered with nuts. Billie had said she'd cook for the Mathis family today.

The rain stopped and the sun broke through the clouds and shone through Amber's kitchen window. A car honked nearby. She leafed through the phone book until she found Mark Petersen's number. He lived on Oak Drive, not far away from her. Should she call or take a chance and surprise him at home? Surprise was always better.

She changed into jeans and a light blue blouse, pushed her feet into flat sandals and buckled them, then grabbed her purse and ran to her car.

Mina drove in as she drove out. Amber waved and Mina frowned. Amber chuckled. Mina hated not knowing what was going on.

On Oak Drive she slowed to read the house numbers. The homes were small, but nice in a subdivision that had been built about ten years ago.

She found the number and started to turn into the drive, then stopped when she saw a long white car. It was Yvonne's Cadillac! Amber pulled away from the house and parked along the street about half a block away. Did Quinn know that Yvonne was seeing Mark Petersen?

Amber's heart raced as she slipped from her car and walked back toward Mark's house. A gentle wind blew her red hair away from her flushed face. She clutched her purse as butterflies fluttered in her stomach. Maybe she'd find some answers today.

She peeked in Mark's open garage. His burgundy Chevy, some garden tools and a trash can were inside. She peeked in the car windows, then looked around. Carefully she lifted the lid on the trash can to see a brown plastic trash bag. Should she look inside? She wrinkled her nose, then twisted the long yellow fastener off. Smells of rotted food hit her and she turned her head and gagged. Cans bumped against each other and a broken glass tinkled as it fell further down into the bag. She should've given this job to Mina.

Amber grinned at the thought as she nudged the garbage. There was nothing that looked important. So much for garbage giving answers.

She crept around the side of Mark's house and stopped near a large bush where no one could spot her and wonder what she was doing. She bit her bottom lip and slowly walked to the protection of another bush. She heard voices. She stopped with her head up and listened. The door leading to a small patio stood open. Mark and Yvonne were out of sight inside, but Amber could hear them easily.

"You *have* to go tonight, Mark." Yvonne's voice was sharp.

"I don't want to. His cards are marked somehow and I never win."

"Take your own deck. You know if you play tonight, you're sure to win. The law of averages say you can't lose every time."

"I don't know about that." Mark's voice was gruff. "I should never have played poker with Wilkens! The stakes are too high."

"It's too late to think about that now."

Amber pressed closer to the bush. A twig stabbed into her arm. A bee buzzed past and she ducked. She knew Mark had a motive for taking money from Ardetts. But that didn't make him a killer. She had to learn more.

"I'll see you later tonight, Mark. Just before ten. I must get going now."

"Are you going to see Quinn Mathis again?" His voice was sharp.

"It's none of your business."

"Don't go out with him. You said you loved me. I hate it when I think of the two of you together."

"You said you'd have a lot of money for us, and you don't. I can't sit still and grow old while I wait for you to get money for us."

"Don't do this to me, Yvonne! I would have had money, but I lost it. And the money I do have I can't spend yet. People would notice and ask questions."

"Don't whine! I'll call you later tonight." Yvonne's voice drifted away and Amber slipped to the side of the bush to hide. Yvonne dare not see her.

The front door slammed and Yvonne walked to her car, her heels tapping on the sidewalk. She drove away without a backward glance. Amber dabbed perspiration off her forehead and upper lip. Before she could slip away, Mark stepped out his back door and stood on the patio with his hands in his pockets, his shoulders bent. As long as he stood there she couldn't move or he'd see her. Frantically she looked around. A fence blocked the way for her to slip into the neighbor's yard.

With a ragged sigh Mark walked to a bench and lowered his lanky frame to it. The wind ruffled his thinning hair. His back was to Amber and she debated whether to sneak away or stay until he went inside. She took a deep breath to steady her nerves and ran lightly on the soft grass to cover the sound of her footsteps. When she reached the front sidewalk, she slowed to a walk to avoid suspicion and walked to her car.

Several minutes later she drove away from Oak Drive. Mark and Yvonne were guilty of gambling, but maybe not of murder. Neither seemed capable of murder. Was someone else involved?

At nine she drove downtown and parked so she could watch Wilkens' Appliance Store. Maybe she could get inside and find out something more.

A car honked and she jumped, then laughed nervously. Street lights brightened the nearly-empty parking lot. Advertising lights flashed off and on. A light glowed inside the appliance store. Everything looked deserted. A carload of boys whipped around the parking lot, then drove away with a blare of their horn.

She ran to the door of Wilkens' store and tried to open it but it was locked. She glanced quickly around, then tried the wooden door beside the plate-glass window. It opened easily and she slipped inside. Cigar smoke hung in the air. In the dim light of the narrow hallway she saw two doors. Also at the far end of the hall was a door with an exit sign over it. If anyone opened a door she'd be trapped. She tiptoed to the first door and listened. It sounded empty and she tried the knob. It didn't turn. She walked to the next door and, when she didn't hear anything, turned the knob but it was locked too.

"Now what?" she muttered.

Just then from inside she heard men's voices. She took a deep breath and knocked three times, waited and knocked once. If the secret knock had changed since Steve's note she would be in big trouble.

The door opened and two men stood there.

She stepped into the room and said in a loud voice, "Well, I'm here and I'm ready for a serious game. What's the holdup? Didn't somebody tell me the game was to start at nine?"

Molly parked in the far corner of the parking lot across from Wilkens'. She had overheard Quinn talking on the phone about finding the answer tonight at Wilkens' Appliance Store. She tried to talk to him before he left, but he said he'd see her in the morning. She looked around for his car but didn't see it. A burgundy Chevy drove up and parked across the lot from her. She ducked down and peered out in time to see Mark Petersen and Yvonne Stoddard walk to Wilkens' and slip inside a wooden door next to the plate-glass window. Her heart hammered as she slipped from her car. Could she walk through the door without being stopped?

Seconds later she reached for the doorknob, butterflies fluttering in her stomach. Suddenly a hand gripped her arm and she turned with a gasp to look up into Quinn's angry face.

"What are you doing here?" he growled as he whisked her down the sidewalk to a small black car. He pushed her into the back seat and slipped in beside her. "Start talking, lady!"

"I . . . I heard you mention that you were coming here. I want to help you."

He buried his fingers in her curls. "Do you know how I felt when I saw you walk to that door? Why didn't you stay home where you belong?"

She saw the strain around his eyes. "Quinn, when will you learn that I am a reporter? I find out the truth about the news. I can't sit at home where it's snug and safe.

He was quiet several seconds, then he sighed. "I don't suppose you'd get in your car and drive away and leave this to me."

She shook her head.

"I didn't think so." He twisted around to watch her and the door. "Well, you're here now. I can't trust you to drive home and wait for me."

She laughed softly. "That sounds inviting."

"Stop it! This is serious business. I'm about to catch the person who killed my brother and his wife."

He slipped from the car and she followed him into the dimly lit hallway. Loud voices came from a closed door. Quinn glanced at his watch, then knocked three times, waited and knocked once.

A cigar in his mouth, Al Wilkens opened the door, saw them and tried to slam it closed, but Quinn was bigger and stronger. He pushed both the door and the man back.

"Get out of here," snapped Al Wilkens.

"I came for answers," said Quinn.

Molly glanced around and gasped when she saw Amber. Amber lifted her brow, but didn't speak.

Yvonne jumped up. "Don't you dare print a word about this, Molly DuPree!"

Mark Petersen buried his face in his hands and groaned.

Quinn slammed the door and stood against it, barring the way. Amber jumped up and barred the other door. Quinn looked at her in surprise. "I'm here to find the truth from Mark Petersen," she said.

Molly moved closer to Quinn.

Yvonne shook her finger at Amber. "Just who are you?"

"Amber Ainslie."

"What?" shrieked Yvonne.

"Private detective," said Amber as if Yvonne hadn't interrupted.

Yvonne sat down beside Mark. Al Wilkens swore. The other two men shook their heads.

"Hired by Mrs. Mathis to learn the truth about the missing money from Ardetts," continued Amber.

"I'll be," said Quinn.

Molly shivered.

"I didn't have nothing to do with Ardetts' money," snapped Al Wilkens.

"Sit down!" barked Quinn.

Al Wilkens hesitated, then dropped to an empty chair.

Amber narrowed her eyes. "Mark?"

He looked up, his face white.

"Don't say anything," snapped Yvonne.

"Mark, I know you lost money gambling," said Amber. "I know you have access to Ardetts' books and money."

"So did Steve Mathis," snapped Yvonne.

"But Steve didn't take the money," said Quinn gruffly.

"No, he didn't," said Amber. "I have proof." Once again she looked at Mark. "I saw you sneak into Steve's study at his home and I know you were looking for records that Steve kept on gambling debts as well as who gambled. I found that notebook and it proves that Steve did not take the money. You did, Mark, and Steve knew it. You know how meticulous he was in keeping notes. He wrote down when he intended to tell the police and that he gave you a chance to turn yourself in. He was going to hand the notebook over to the authorities and you killed him before he could."

Mark shook his head and whispered, "No, no, no."

"You were seen sneaking around the parking lot during the party the night of the accident," said Amber. "You also broke into the appliance store to steal back your IOU, but you didn't get it."

"I thought it might be you." Al Wilkens shook a fat finger at Mark. "You're nothing but trouble!"

"*You* killed my brother!" growled Quinn, glaring at Mark.

"No!" Mark cried.

"Yes, you did," said Amber grimly.

"It was Yvonne's idea to fix the brakes!" cried Mark. "I didn't mean for anyone to die. I just wanted to scare Steve into giving me that notebook."

Quinn growled deep in his throat and Molly slipped her hand through his arm to comfort him.

One of the men at the table stood up. "That's all I need. I'm Sergeant Martin, F.P.D. Mark Petersen, Yvonne Stoddard, Al Wilkens, you're all three under arrest."

"Let's go home," said Molly later, gently tugging Quinn's arm.

He nodded, his face gray and his eyes haunted. They walked onto the street just in time to see the police car drive away, its lights flashing.

Amber held her hand out to Quinn. "I hope you forgive my intrusion into your home, Quinn."

He shook her hand stiffly. "I do. I feel badly that

168

my mother couldn't trust me enough to tell me about you."

"She'll explain." Amber smiled. "I'll report to her in the morning and she can have Bella come back to work." She turned to Molly. "Thanks for your help."

Molly nodded. "Any time."

Amber ran across the street to her car. She knew Mina would be waiting for a report.

"Follow me home, Molly," Quinn said in a tired voice.

She nodded.

Later at home she stopped him in the grassy yard. Moonlight streamed down, lighting a silvery path across the yard. "Are you all right?"

"I will be."

"Now you know the truth about Steve. He really was working to prove that Mark took the money from Ardetts."

Quinn nodded. "How about a cup of coffee before you go to your room? I want to tell you something important."

She hesitated, then followed him to the kitchen where Billie had left coffee sitting beside the stove, the red button on to show it was hot. The look on Quinn's face sent her heart racing.

He filled two cups and handed one to her. She sat at the table without putting in cream or sugar. The dog barked outdoors and the house creaked.

"Molly, I had a call from Jan today. She and Neville will be home next week. It seems that Mother knew you wouldn't be with us for six months and called Jan to see if they could hurry their business."

Molly moved restlessly.

"If you want, you can pack and go back to town tonight or you can wait until morning."

She stared at him in horror. "What?"

"Isn't that what you want?"

"No! I mean, I can stay until they get here."

He shook his head. "Under the circumstances I would prefer you leave now."

She faced him where he stood at the sink. "What circumstances, Quinn?"

"You. Me. You know."

"I don't know!"

"You're ruining my life."

Pain squeezed her heart. "Ruining it? Are you afraid you can't control your emotions with me here?"

Anger leapt in his eyes. "You rate yourself too high, Molly."

She shrugged, but the words had stung. "Then you have nothing to fear."

"I am not afraid of a frizzy-headed girl who wastes years planning a wedding to a man she doesn't love."

She fell back, her hand to her heart.

"Sorry."

Suddenly she realized what he was doing. He did find her attractive and was afraid he'd fall in love with her. She stepped toward him. "I'll make a deal with you, Quinn."

"From the look in your eyes I know I won't like it."

"We'll set up a system." She laughed and he frowned. "It's quite simple. If I can't keep my hands off you, I'll warn you and you can flee. You do the same. Only I might find it more enjoyable to stay and see what happens."

"Very funny." He plunked his cup down.

"Do you agree?"

"Get out of here!"

She laughed. "Why?"

He strode to the door, then turned. "This is good-bye, Molly."

He was serious! "No!"

"Yes," he whispered hoarsely. "It's better this way."

She ran to him, but he held her away. "I can't leave now. It's too soon, Quinn. What about the girls?"

"I told them today. They'll miss you, but they're looking forward to Jan and Neville coming for them. And they'll have Billie."

Molly backed away, her face pale and her eyes haunted. "Goodbye then. Will I see you again sometime?"

"No. It's better if we don't see each other again." He shook his head and pushed through the door. The silence enveloped her and crushed her and she sagged against a counter. He really didn't love her, not even a little. How could she live without him? He was her life!

For the next several days she stayed in her apartment, sobbing into her pillow. Food stuck in her throat. She had written the article about Mark and Yvonne and Al Wilkens but had found no pleasure in it.

Molly stood at her bay window and watched a robin hopping in the grass. Listlessly she walked to the bathroom and splashed cold water on her face. She frowned. Was that pale, washed-out girl really Molly DuPree, fighter, survivor, famous reporter?

"Molly, this is it! You can't go on like this!"

In a flash she brushed on blush and applied eye makeup to hide the pain she felt. She dressed in a rose-colored dress with short sleeves and flaring skirt. She tightened the belt and slipped her feet into high-heeled sandals. Once again she was Molly DuPree, the beautiful butterfly. She smiled but it didn't reach her eyes.

The doorbell rang and she jumped, then frowned. Was it Amber? She said she might be over today.

Molly opened the door, then gasped as Quinn pushed his way in. He wore a light blue suit and white shirt without a tie. He looked hot and tense.

"It's not working, Molly!"

She stood before him, trembling. "What isn't?"

"You fill my thoughts constantly! I had a meeting with our supervisors today and Mother had to take over. I couldn't remember what I was saying. Do you know how humiliating that is?"

"Why did you come here?" Did he want her to vanish from the face of the earth?

"I had notes right in front of me, but I kept forgetting what I was saying." He paced across the small living room like a caged lion.

"Oh?" Was he here to tell her that he couldn't live without her? She smiled and her eyes twinkled.

"Yes, I forgot!" He gripped her arms. "And it's not at all funny.,"

"I wasn't laughing." But a bubble of happiness burst inside her and she couldn't hide the laughter on her face.

He buried his face in her wild curls. "What have you done to me? Why can't I get you out of my head?"

She slid her arms under his jacket and around his waist. "Maybe you don't really want to."

"I want to." he held her away, his eyes haunted. "How do I know I can really trust you?"

"You can't mean that!"

"You fooled me once before."

"Never again, Quinn!"

"You ruined my life!"

"Love doesn't ruin. It builds."

He held her close and she felt his heart pounding against hers, blending with her wild heartbeats. His special aroma sent her senses racing.

"Do you love me, Molly?" He asked huskily, his cheek pressed against hers.

She hesitated, afraid to say the words aloud. If he rejected her after the words were spoken, she could not survive. But she had to take the chance. She moved so that she could look into his emotion-filled eyes. She cupped her hand along the side of his sun darkened face and felt him tremble. "I love you, Quinn. I love you with a burning passion that grows stronger every minute that I'm near you."

The last word was smothered as he kissed her. She clung to him, glorying in his touch. The kiss consumed her. Finally he lifted his head and the haggard, haunted look was replaced with a look that melted her very bones.

"I love you, Molly. I love you!"

"Oh, Quinn! I was afraid I'd never hear you say it." She pulled his face down and showered it with kisses. "I love you."

His lips covered hers in a kiss that left no room for words. "When can you marry me, Molly? Tomorrow?"

"Tomorrow! Any time you say, Quinn."